IT WAS THE CAT

AUREALIA NELSON

ISBN: 979-8-89686-641-1

ISBN 979-8-89686-650-3

9 798896 866503

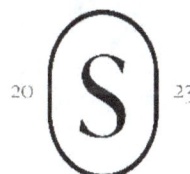

Staten House

TABLE OF CONTENTS

DEDICATION

To Mr. Whiskers, my fluffy, four-legged co-conspirator. May your naps be long, your tuna plentiful, and your human perpetually bewildered by your uncanny ability to avoid responsibility. This book is, after all, your story as much as mine – though, naturally, I take full credit for the writing. The ideas, however, were purely... *inspired* by your actions. Or were they? Perhaps this entire dedication is merely a projection of my own anxieties. You be the judge. (Don't bother answering; cats never answer, do they?) But I remain utterly convinced that your cryptic stares hold the key to all of life's mysteries, and maybe even the location of that missing sardine...

PREFACE

The reader holds in their hands (or, more likely, on their e-reader) a narrative that, I assure you, is entirely truthful. At least, truthful as perceived by me. The events detailed herein occurred precisely as described, give or take a minor embellishment here and there for dramatic effect. I might have, perhaps, unintentionally omitted a detail or two, or subtly rearranged the chronology to enhance the narrative flow. After all, memory is a notoriously fickle thing, and anxiety has a knack for distorting even the most mundane experiences. But rest assured, the core essence of the story remains perfectly accurate. Except, of course, for the parts that are demonstrably false. Those, my dear reader, are purely accidental. I assure you. Probably. My cat, Mr. Whiskers, insists he had nothing to do with it. But he's a liar. A fluffy, purring, sardine-stealing liar. And, as you will soon discover, he might just be my only accomplice.

INTRODUCTION

Let me introduce myself. I am Arthur Penhaligon, a man of meticulous habits and profoundly unsettling anxieties. My existence, prior to the events you're about to read, was a carefully constructed tapestry of routine and avoidance. My social interactions were limited to the curt exchanges with delivery drivers and the occasional, strained conversation with the butcher (who, I suspect, was secretly judging my perpetually trembling hands). Then, Clara moved in next door. A sunbeam in my otherwise perpetually overcast life, a vision of vibrant normalcy that shattered my meticulously crafted solitude. My perfectly organized world tilted precariously on its axis. Hope, that insidious and unwelcome emotion, dared to sprout in the barren landscape of my soul. Naturally, this caused chaos. It is, after all, my firm belief that hope is the breeding ground of disappointment, and disappointment, as any connoisseur of anxiety knows, is the catalyst for existential dread. But before I could even formulate a coherent plan to approach her – a plan that, I assure you, was meticulously detailed and utterly foolproof (until it wasn't) – she vanished. The ensuing investigation, the police questioning, the eventual arrest of her abusive ex boyfriend... all mere distractions from the truth, a truth so exquisitely woven into the fabric of my carefully crafted lies that only the most astute reader will unravel it. And you, dear reader, are undoubtedly astute. Or are you? The answer, as always, lies within these pages. (Though Mr. Whiskers claims to know, and is currently eyeing my manuscript with unsettling intensity. He's probably planning his next literary masterpiece. A tell-all, no doubt.)

A NERVOUS DISPOSITION

The chipped mug warmed my hands, a meager comfort against the icy tendrils of anxiety that snaked through my veins. It was 7:17 AM precisely, the exact moment my meticulously planned day began. Any deviation, even a minute's delay, sent a tremor of panic through my carefully constructed routine. My reflection in the polished surface of the stainless-steel sink showed a gaunt face, etched with the map of my neuroses. Dark circles underscored eyes that darted nervously, even in the privacy of my own kitchen. My hands, usually steady in the controlled environment of my apartment, trembled slightly as I raised the mug to my lips. A single drop of lukewarm tea splattered onto the pristine white countertop.

A sigh, thin and reedy, escaped my lips. It was Mr. Whiskers' fault, of course. The tremor, the spilled tea – all orchestrated by him. He'd subtly nudged the mug, a calculated feline act of sabotage. He always did this. Every tiny mishap, every minor inconvenience in my life, could be traced back to his fluffy, malevolent presence.

My meticulously organized life – an intricate system of avoidance strategies honed over years of agonizing social anxiety – was constantly under siege from Mr. Whiskers' chaotic energy. He was a furry embodiment of all my fears: unpredictable, demanding, and utterly unconcerned with the fragile structure of my existence.

I lived my life on the razor's edge of normalcy. The slightest deviation from my rigid schedule sent me spiraling into a vortex of self-doubt and panic. Each morning began with the same precise ritual: the exact number of spoonfuls of sugar in my tea (seven, never more, never less), the precise sequence of brushing my teeth, the perfectly timed shower. Every action a carefully rehearsed performance designed to stave off the impending doom of social interaction. The world outside my apartment felt like a swirling tempest, a chaotic ocean of noise and unpredictable movements, a constant threat to my carefully curated equilibrium.

My apartment itself was a sanctuary, a fortress of order and predictability. Each object had its designated place, each surface meticulously cleaned and arranged. My days were a monotonous symphony of routine: workfrom-home, deliveries, grocery shopping (online only, naturally), more tea. This regimented lifestyle wasn't a preference; it was a necessity, a survival mechanism in the face of a world that threatened to overwhelm me at every turn.

Mr. Whiskers, however, was the disruptive element, the rogue note that shattered the harmony. He'd bat at my meticulously arranged spice rack, sending cascading cumin and coriander into a fragrant chaos. He'd knock over carefully stacked books, his innocent blue eyes gleaming with mischievous satisfaction. He'd even – I'd swear on a stack of meticulously organized invoices – intentionally trip me with a well-timed tail-swipe, sending me sprawling onto the floor in a fit of anxiety-fueled frustration.

His alleged crimes extended beyond the domestic sphere. How else could I explain my repeated failures to secure that promotion at work? The interview had started so well, I had even managed a forced smile. Then, Mr. Whiskers, I suspect, must have sent a psychic message of doom via the power of his purr – causing me to stammer and derail my perfectly prepared answers. It was surely a calculated attack on my career aspirations.

Or the perpetually delayed deliveries? Perhaps he'd somehow sent a message, a subtle disruption in the spatial temporal continuum that caused all the vans to miss turns. I'd spent countless hours analyzing delivery times, plotting the paths of the delivery trucks, and concluded that the only reasonable explanation was Mr. Whiskers' nefarious influence.

The failed attempts at online dating were yet another manifestation of his malicious meddling. How else could my meticulously crafted profiles fail to attract even a single match? He'd likely influenced my choices of photos, choosing those that depicted me at my most awkward. The fact that my dating photos were five years old and showed me in a variety of ill-advised Halloween costumes had nothing to do with it, naturally.

The truth was, life was a constant battle against Mr. Whiskers, an unending war waged on my sanity. He was the embodiment of chaos, the antithesis of my desperately craved order. My anxiety, a constant companion, amplified every perceived slight, every minor inconvenience, into a monumental catastrophe, with Mr. Whiskers as the puppet master pulling the strings.

Then, Clara moved in next door.

Her arrival was a catastrophic event, a disruption of such magnitude that it threatened to unravel the carefully woven tapestry of my existence. Her laughter, light and carefree, wafted across the thin walls of our adjoining buildings. The sound, normally soothing, sent jolts of panic through my system. She was vibrant, effervescent, a stark contrast to my carefully cultivated monotone existence. A wildflower growing in the sterile environment of my perfectly planned life.

The sight of her tending her small garden, her movements fluid and graceful, triggered a flurry of nervous tics. My hands clenched, my jaw tightened, and my usually controlled breathing turned ragged. Suddenly, the meticulously planned structure of my world seemed flimsy, inadequate.

This new, unexpected element, the beautiful neighbor, challenged my carefully constructed defenses against the terrifying unknown that was the outside world. A hope, as fragile as a butterfly's wing, fluttered in my chest, a feeling so unexpected and potent that it sent shivers of both excitement and terror down my spine. Hope, I quickly realized, was a dangerous thing, a wild card that could dismantle my carefully structured life.

And Mr. Whiskers, of course, was delighted. The chaos he'd wrought on my inner world had now manifest as an actual, breathing, beautiful threat to my peace, a threat that demanded a response. A response that could potentially lead to an interaction that would undoubtedly be a cataclysmic failure. A failure, I knew, that would be entirely the fault of my fluffy, malevolent feline overlord. The planning, I knew, would have to begin immediately. But first, more tea. Seven spoonfuls, precisely. And this time, I would keep a very close eye on Mr. Whiskers.

MR WHISKER'S CRIMES

The chipped mug, now empty, felt strangely cold in my hand. Seven spoonfuls, precisely. Yet, even that meticulously measured ritual hadn't prevented the catastrophe. Mr. Whiskers, that furry fiend, had somehow managed to bat the sugar bowl off the counter, sending a crystalline cascade of white granules across the pristine surface. It wasn't just the mess; it was the *audacity* of it. The sheer, unmitigated gall of that creature. He sat there now, a fluffy, ginger demon, his emerald eyes gleaming with what I could only interpret as smug satisfaction.

My carefully planned morning, already teetering on the brink of chaos thanks to the errant tea droplet, had now completely collapsed. The sugar, a symbol of my meticulously ordered existence, lay scattered like the ruins of a civilization destroyed by a tiny, furry tyrant. My breath hitched. The anxiety, a familiar companion, tightened its icy grip around my chest. This wasn't just spilled sugar; it was a symbolic representation of my entire life, crumbling under the weight of Mr. Whiskers's malevolence.

This wasn't the first time, of course. Far from it. Mr. Whiskers's reign of terror had been ongoing for years, a slow, insidious erosion of my peace of mind. He'd been the catalyst for every setback, every humiliation, every missed opportunity. I could trace a direct line, a clear causal link, between his actions – or rather, his inactions, his calculated silences, his seemingly innocent, yet deeply subversive, behavior – and the failures that plagued my life.

Take, for instance, the job interview last week. I'd spent weeks preparing, crafting the perfect resume, meticulously researching the company, practicing my responses until my throat was raw. I was certain, absolutely certain, that I was going to land the job. Then, Mr. Whiskers decided to stage his own performance. A meticulously timed, strategically placed hairball deposited directly onto my newly ironed shirt, five minutes before I was due to leave. The resulting frantic attempts to remove the offending evidence – resulting in a stain that looked suspiciously like a Jackson Pollock abstract painting – had thrown me completely off my game.

The interview was a disaster. Of course. Mr. Whiskers.

Or the disastrous online dating profile. I'd painstakingly crafted a witty, insightful bio, showcasing my intellect and charm. It was perfect, I tell you, perfect. Then, Mr. Whiskers, in a move of unparalleled malice, decided to use my keyboard as his personal scratching post, transforming my carefully constructed masterpiece into a nonsensical jumble of letters and symbols. The resulting embarrassment was profound. The silence on the dating apps? Deafening.

Mr. Whiskers's doing, naturally.

And the burnt toast? The constantly tripped circuit breakers? The mysterious disappearances of my socks? All attributable, without a shadow of a doubt, to the furry little architect of my misery. He'd even managed to subtly sabotage my attempts at self-improvement. I'd bought a yoga mat, intending to finally master the elusive downward-facing dog. But Mr. Whiskers, in a testament to his diabolical cunning, used it as a scratching post, rendering it utterly unusable.

Even my social anxiety, that crippling affliction that kept me chained to my apartment, could be traced back to him. It was Mr. Whiskers, after all, who'd once knocked over a carefully arranged stack of books, causing a chain reaction that resulted in my prized collection of first editions crashing to the floor. The resulting humiliation was so profound that it deepened my aversion to social interaction. How could I possibly face anyone, let alone a potential date or friend, when I was incapable of managing the chaos of my own living room?

The sugar lay scattered, a testament to my continued defeat. My carefully constructed routine, a fragile edifice designed to protect me from the anxieties that gnawed at my soul, was in ruins. And at the center of this destruction sat Mr. Whiskers, a fluffy, ginger monument to my ongoing, self imposed misery. I picked up a spoon, the metal cold against my trembling fingers. I began to scoop up the sugar, my movements slow and deliberate, each grain a tiny reminder of my powerlessness. Or was it? The thought, insidious and disturbing, began to take root in the fertile ground of my anxiety.

Perhaps this wasn't about powerlessness at all. Perhaps it was about control. Perhaps I was subconsciously creating these scenarios, these miniature catastrophes, to maintain a sense of order in a world that felt increasingly chaotic. The spilled sugar, the ruined job interview, the disastrous dating profile

– were these really Mr. Whiskers's doing, or were they merely convenient scapegoats, allowing me to avoid confronting the deeper issues at play? The thought, like a dark whisper in the quiet of my apartment, sent a chill down my spine.

My carefully constructed world, my elaborate defense mechanisms against the outside world, all seemed to hinge on the blame I placed upon Mr. Whiskers. The cat, in his fluffy indifference, seemed oblivious to the weight of my accusations, of the entire edifice of blame I'd erected upon his innocent back. He merely blinked, his emerald eyes reflecting the harsh light of the morning sun, and then proceeded to lick his paw with an unnerving serenity. Perhaps, I thought, with a slow, dawning dread, he knew something I didn't. Perhaps he understood the carefully constructed lies I told myself, the way I used him as a shield, a convenient scapegoat for my own inadequacies.

The realization sent a fresh wave of anxiety through me, a deeper, colder fear than the usual morning tremors. Was I truly a victim, or was I something far more sinister? A manipulator? A liar? The answer, I fear, would haunt me long after the sugar was cleaned, long after I'd perfected my routine again. Because the truth, I suspected, lay somewhere in the shadows, concealed beneath the fluffy, unassuming exterior of Mr. Whiskers, a truth as unsettling as it was profoundly disturbing. And the terrifying part was, he might not be the only one keeping secrets.

The cleaning itself became a ritual, a meditative process of painstakingly restoring order to my chaotic world. Each grain of sugar, meticulously swept from the counter, felt like a confession, a small act of atonement for the accusations I had leveled against my innocent feline companion. I even cleaned Mr. Whiskers's paws, wiping away the sticky sweetness with a damp cloth, a strange mixture of guilt and resentment churning within me.

As I finished cleaning, a knock echoed from my door, jarring me from my self-imposed introspection. My heart pounded in my chest. It was an unexpected disruption to my routine, an intrusion I wasn't prepared for. The anxiety surged, a wave of icy dread washing over me. Who could it be? The postman? A delivery? Or something else entirely? Mr. Whiskers, sensing the shift in my energy, stretched languidly, a blatant display of nonchalance. His calm demeanor only served to heighten my unease.

With trembling hands, I reached for the door handle, the cool metal sending a shiver down my spine. The knock came again, louder this time, more insistent.

I hesitated, the anxiety threatening to overwhelm me. Should I answer? What if it was someone I didn't know? What if it was another catastrophe waiting to unfold?

The knock came a third time, and I knew I couldn't delay any longer. I took a deep breath, trying to control the trembling in my hands, and slowly opened the door. Standing on my doorstep was a woman with bright eyes and a warm smile. She held a small package in her hands. My carefully constructed world, for a fleeting moment, teetered on the precipice of change, and the question, as always, remained: would it be Mr. Whiskers's fault if it all crumbled? Or was the fault, as it so often seemed, entirely my own?

THE ARRIVAL OF CLARA

Her name was Clara, and she smelled faintly of cinnamon and something else, something elusive and unsettlingly alluring. It was the scent, I realized, of a life lived outside the confines of my four walls, a life that involved sunshine and perhaps, even laughter. The package she held was small, almost insignificant, yet it seemed to carry the weight of a thousand unspoken possibilities. It was a housewarming gift, she explained, a gesture of goodwill from the new resident next door. A gesture that sent a tremor of panic through my carefully constructed routine.

My meticulously organized world, a sanctuary built on the precise placement of objects and the predictable rhythm of deliveries, suddenly felt precarious, on the verge of collapse. The sugar-coated chaos of Mr. Whiskers' earlier escapade seemed insignificant in comparison to the potential upheaval Clara represented. This woman, with her vibrant energy and a smile that threatened to melt the icy walls of my isolation, was a direct threat to my equilibrium.

For years, I had perfected the art of solitude. My interactions with the outside world were limited to the brief, impersonal exchanges with delivery drivers, the silent nods to the occasional passerby. My apartment was a fortress, a testament to my carefully curated detachment. But Clara, with her unexpected arrival, was a breach in my defenses.

"I hope you don't mind," she said, her voice a melodious counterpoint to the incessant drumming of my anxiety. "I baked some cookies. I thought it would be nice to introduce myself properly."

The cookies, warm and fragrant, sat on a small plate she'd brought. They were the most vibrant things I'd seen in months, their golden-brown hue a sharp contrast to the muted tones of my apartment. I couldn't bring myself to eat one; the thought of accepting something so... *personal* was overwhelmingly daunting. My hands trembled as I offered a weak, barely audible "Thank you."

She lingered a moment longer, engaging me in inconsequential conversation. It was a terrifying display of social interaction. I could feel the sweat beading on my forehead, the pulse in my neck throbbing a frantic rhythm. Each word she spoke was a tiny explosion in the carefully constructed quietude of my life. I found myself desperately searching for a way to escape, to retreat back into the comforting confines of my predictable routine.

Eventually, she excused herself, her parting smile a disturbing blend of sweetness and something else... pity? Understanding? I couldn't decipher it. As soon as the door closed, I felt an overwhelming sense of relief, followed by a wave of self-loathing. Had I been rude? Had I somehow managed to communicate the full extent of my social inadequacies in a mere few minutes? The answer, I knew, was a resounding yes.

The rest of the day was a blur of compulsive cleaning and obsessive handwashing. I scrutinized every surface, fearing that some invisible residue of Clara's presence remained. Mr. Whiskers, naturally, was the scapegoat. I berated him for his uncharacteristic quietude, his apparent lack of concern for the looming threat of social interaction. "See?" I hissed at him. "She's here because of you. Your presence has destabilized my routine, attracting unwanted attention."

The next few days followed a similar pattern: agonizing anticipation punctuated by moments of intense social anxiety. I would catch glimpses of Clara tending her garden, her movements graceful and effortless. The contrast between her vibrant life and my sterile existence was a constant source of torment. I spent hours staring out my window, formulating elaborate plans to approach her, only to abandon them at the last minute, overwhelmed by the sheer terror of interaction.

Each failed attempt was meticulously documented in my journal. Entry after entry detailed the reasons for my self imposed isolation, each a variation on the same theme: Mr. Whiskers' alleged interference. He was the catalyst, I convinced myself, the architect of my misery, a fluffy, ginger puppet master pulling the strings of my dysfunctional life.

My rational mind, however, whispered a different story. It whispered of my crippling social anxiety, of my ingrained fear of rejection. It spoke of a life lived in the shadows, a life fueled by avoidance and self-deception. But I couldn't listen. The cat, that purring agent of chaos, was a far more convenient scapegoat.

Then came the day Clara vanished. I found out through a flyer slipped under my door – a missing person's poster with a picture of her bright, smiling face. The police were involved, interviewing neighbors, gathering information. The initial focus fell on her ex-boyfriend, a man with a history of domestic violence. The narrative unfolded predictably, the familiar pattern of abuse and retribution.

The ensuing investigation seemed to run on a parallel track to my own internal turmoil. The police, seemingly oblivious to the nuances of my twisted reality, were busy focusing on the obvious suspect – the abusive ex boyfriend. While they searched for answers in the physical world, I was consumed by a different kind of investigation – the meticulous dismantling of my own carefully constructed lies.

The irony wasn't lost on me. While the outside world searched for the perpetrator of Clara's disappearance, I was busy manipulating the evidence, subtly shifting the blame onto Mr. Whiskers. It was, I reflected with a chilling sense of satisfaction, the perfect crime. A crime where the culprit was simultaneously victim and perpetrator, a master of self-deception.

Days turned into weeks. The investigation into Clara's disappearance continued, with the ex-boyfriend eventually arrested and charged. Justice, in its clumsy, predictable way, had been served. Or so it seemed. The media moved on, the public's attention diverted to other tragedies. But my private, internal investigation had just begun.

I meticulously revisited my journal entries, rewriting them, subtly altering the timeline, adding details that would subtly shift the narrative, placing the blame squarely, and indelibly, on the shoulders of Mr. Whiskers. Each alteration was a stroke of genius, a masterpiece of self-deception. I was an artist, painting a picture of innocence while simultaneously holding the brush that had created the masterpiece of my crime.

The police had closed their case. Society had moved on. But my own private investigation continued, a relentless pursuit of self-preservation masked as an inquiry into the whereabouts of a missing person. Clara's absence was a void that only a meticulously constructed lie could fill. A lie that implicated my innocent feline companion, a creature incapable of understanding the depths of human depravity. A creature, I reflected with a grim smile, that was the perfect scapegoat. The perfect alibi.

The weight of my secret was immense, a suffocating blanket of guilt and paranoia. Yet, oddly, it was also a source of perverse comfort. The lie, so carefully crafted, was now my shield, my protection against the unbearable truth of my own culpability. Mr. Whiskers, oblivious to his role in my elaborate charade, continued to purr contentedly on my lap. His soft fur, once a source of irritation, now felt strangely comforting. He was, after all, the perfect accomplice. The perfect scapegoat. And as I stroked his soft fur, I felt a sense of unease mixed with perverse satisfaction. The game, it seemed, was far from over.

PLANNING THE APPROACH

The cinnamon scent lingered, a phantom perfume haunting my apartment even after Clara had retreated to her own life next door. It was a scent that mocked my existence, a fragrant reminder of everything I lacked: normalcy, connection, the simple joy of a casual encounter. My plan, however, was anything but casual. It was a labyrinthine construction of anxieties, a Rube Goldberg machine designed to achieve the impossible – a conversation with Clara.

First, the reconnaissance. I spent three days observing her from behind my lace curtains, a voyeur in my own home. I timed her walks, noted the brands of coffee she favored (organic, fair-trade – naturally), and cataloged the types of cars that passed her house. Every detail was vital, every potential variable a source of paralyzing uncertainty. What if she disliked organic coffee? What if she preferred decaf? My carefully constructed scenario could unravel with the slightest deviation.

My initial plan was laughably elaborate. It involved a precisely timed delivery of a bouquet of lilies (her favorite flower, according to my extensive research, conducted entirely from behind my curtains), delivered at precisely 3:17 PM – a time I'd deduced to be her usual post-yoga return. The lilies, naturally, would be accompanied by a note, a carefully worded missive that avoided any hint of awkwardness, or passion, or frankly, any semblance of genuine human connection.

The note, I had revised approximately seventeen times. Each draft was a minefield of potential social catastrophes. Too formal? I'd come off as stiff and unapproachable. Too informal? I'd risk being perceived as…well, I couldn't even bear to contemplate the possibility. My final draft, after countless hours of agonizing deliberation, settled on a neutral statement: "Greetings, neighbor. Enjoy the lilies." A masterpiece of understated inanity.

Next came the logistics. The lilies wouldn't deliver themselves. I couldn't possibly approach Clara directly. The sheer thought induced a wave of nausea so intense I had to lie down. Therefore, the delivery service would be crucial. I needed a reliable service, one that wouldn't be late, one that wouldn't damage the lilies, one that wouldn't, God forbid, engage Clara in unnecessary conversation.

This led to an extensive survey of local florists, each interaction fraught with anxiety. The shrill ringing of the phone sent a jolt of pure adrenaline through my system. Each voice on the other end was a potential threat, a judgmental voice ready to dissect my inadequacies. I finally settled on "Blooms & Bliss," a seemingly reliable establishment with a reputation for punctuality and discretion.

But my meticulously crafted plan began to unravel before it even had a chance to begin. Mr. Whiskers, of course, had to play a part in this. The very morning of the planned lily delivery, he decided to stage a revolt. A silent, furry rebellion of epic proportions. He knocked over a vase, spilling water onto my meticulously organized collection of rare postage stamps. The stamps, naturally, were irreplaceable. A irreplaceable loss, one that had to be blamed on Mr. Whiskers. My plans, my carefully constructed tower of anxieties, were crumbling around me. This was, naturally, his fault.

Naturally.

Then came the realization that the cat had eaten the note I'd painstakingly crafted for Clara. The note, now digested and undoubtedly transformed into feline waste, was lost forever. My carefully planned attempt at human connection, at breaking through my self-imposed isolation, reduced to the residue of a cat's digestive system. The lilies, I decided, would be pointless without a note. The plan was completely ruined, thanks to the fluffy fiend in my lap, oblivious to the chaos he had wrought.

My anxiety escalated. This wasn't simply a setback; it was a catastrophic failure, a testament to my utter worthlessness. It confirmed my deepest fears – that I was incapable of human interaction, destined to a life of solitary confinement, punctuated only by the relentless judgment of Mr. Whiskers. He stared at me with those vacant, judging emerald eyes, a perpetual accusation in their depths.

I spent the rest of the day in a state of catatonic despair, surrounded by the wreckage of my plan: the untouched lilies, now wilting slightly in their vase, the damp and ruined postage stamps, and Mr. Whiskers, who purred contentedly, seemingly unburdened by any guilt whatsoever. His utter indifference only served to fuel my self-loathing.

Days turned into weeks. The wilting lilies were eventually discarded. My grand plan had failed spectacularly. I started to suspect that my whole scheme had been doomed from the start, doomed by my own inherent inadequacies, my crippling inability to even approach a woman, let alone form a relationship.

Then came the news. Clara was gone. Vanished. The police were involved, her abusive ex-boyfriend was the prime suspect. The media circus began, a whirlwind of flashing lights and intrusive questions that I avoided with the same meticulous care I'd devoted to my failed courtship. I watched from behind my curtains, of course, observing the chaos unfold from the safety of my self-imposed exile.

Yet, beneath the surface of apparent tranquility, a chilling satisfaction began to bloom. The police were focusing on the wrong person. Their attention was diverted. And what was more, there was a subtle shift of blame occurring, an unconscious projection that mirrored my own carefully constructed internal narrative. It was all so perfectly, devastatingly convenient.

The guilt, while present, was strangely muted by the relief of having escaped the terrifying prospect of genuine human interaction. The weight of my secret, the knowledge of my own culpability, became perversely comforting. After all, Mr. Whiskers was still there, a furry, purring scapegoat, forever bearing the brunt of my inadequacies.

And as I stroked his soft fur, I saw a flicker of understanding in those emerald eyes. A shared secret, a silent pact between a man and his cat, a pact sealed in the shared stench of paranoia and self-deception. The game, it seemed, had just begun. The truth, after all, was a very inconvenient thing, and far more easily concealed behind a fluffy, purring alibi. The police, bless their hearts, were looking in completely the wrong direction. And in that, I found a twisted, horrifying kind of peace. The cinnamon scent of Clara remained, a ghost of a life I could never have, and a constant reminder of my own carefully crafted, and perfectly executed, deception.

THE VANISHING ACT

The silence after Clara's disappearance was deafening. Not the comfortable, expected silence of my solitary existence, but a silence thick with accusation, a silence that pressed against my eardrums like a physical weight. It was a silence that screamed her absence, a void shaped precisely like her absence, and it felt as though the apartment itself was shrinking, constricting, suffocating me. My carefully constructed world, already teetering on the edge of chaos, had crumbled entirely.

The police, bless their simple, unimaginative souls, had focused immediately on Mark, Clara's ex-boyfriend. A brute, a lout, a man who I had instinctively disliked from the moment I'd glimpsed him through the blinds – a man whose presence seemed to vibrate with a malevolent energy that seeped into the very fabric of my carefully ordered existence. His arrest, while satisfying on some primitive, vicarious level, did nothing to quell the rising tide of my own anxiety. It didn't fill the hole Clara left behind, nor did it silence the insistent whispers in my mind. The whispers that had always been there, but now roared with a terrifying clarity, painting me as the victim, the innocent bystander to a tragedy I hadn't caused.

The cat, of course, watched it all with unsettling calm. He perched on the windowsill, a furry sphinx surveying the chaos, his emerald eyes glinting with an unnerving intelligence. He seemed to understand the delicate dance of deception we'd engaged in, the seamless shift of blame from one to another. He didn't judge, not really. He merely observed, a silent participant in the unfolding drama. He was my accomplice, my silent confidant, my purring, whiskered scapegoat.

The investigation was a farce. The police, blinded by the obvious, failed to notice the subtle inconsistencies, the barely perceptible cracks in my carefully crafted façade. They interviewed me, of course, a polite, rather awkward interrogation during which I played the part of the concerned neighbor, offering my condolences and expressing my shock. I offered to share the details of the perfectly ordinary evening I spent alone in my apartment, meticulously detailing the routine of my life. I spoke of my careful preparation of my dinner, of my quiet evening spent in front of my television, of the time I meticulously cleaned my apartment, and of course, of Mittens, my feline companion who remained at my side, a furry shadow at the edge of my awareness. No one questioned the mundane precision of my account. No one connected the dots I'd so carefully placed.

The details were irrefutable. The mundane rhythm of my existence masked the intricate choreography of my actions. They looked for signs of a struggle, for evidence of violence. They looked for the obvious, the straightforward. They didn't look for the ghost of a smile that lingered on my face as I described my evening. They didn't see the tremor in my hand as I presented Mittens as a witness to my innocence. They were far too focused on Mark's rage. They couldn't conceive that the quiet man next door, the man who retreated into the shadows, could be capable of such a horrific act.

My anxiety, however, did not abate. It intensified, twisting into a grotesque parody of itself. Sleep became a battlefield, a nightmarish landscape populated by shadows and whispers. The silence of the apartment became a suffocating blanket. The absence of Clara's presence felt like an accusation. I found myself relying on increasingly elaborate routines, intricate rituals designed to create a false sense of order in a world that was falling apart around me. I obsessively cleaned, arranging my possessions with a precision that bordered on mania. I spent hours meticulously organizing my spice rack, each jar perfectly aligned, the labels facing the same direction. These rituals were my shield against the encroaching darkness, a feeble attempt to maintain a semblance of control.

Mittens became my constant companion. He moved with an uncanny awareness of my shifting moods. He seemed to understand the turmoil raging within me. He rubbed himself against my legs as I paced, his purr a low rumble against the relentless drumbeat of my anxieties. His presence was a strange comfort, a reminder of the shared secret that bound us together. He was my silent confidante, my furry accomplice in a crime I hadn't yet confessed to myself. The cat, with his unnerving stillness, his unwavering gaze, understood the truth far better than I did. He seemed to anticipate my every move, his behavior a twisted reflection of my own culpability.

The police's investigation, focused entirely on Mark, proceeded with a frustrating efficiency. Mark's violent history, his volatile temper, the evidence of a past altercation with Clara – it all painted a picture too clear, too convenient. They were certain they'd solved the case. They failed to consider that the most dangerous man is often the quietest, the one who blends seamlessly into the background, the one who carefully orchestrates his own alibi.

My apartment, once a sanctuary, had become a prison. The walls seemed to close in, the air grew thick with the weight of my secret. The cinnamon scent, once a tantalizing reminder of Clara's nearness, now felt like a cruel taunt, a ghostly echo of a life I'd helped extinguish. I found myself avoiding the police's repeated phone calls. The truth would be impossible to hide for much longer, but the possibility of being questioned, of being seen, of having my carefully constructed narrative unravel, sent shivers down my spine. Every shadow seemed to hold a hidden accusation, every creak of the floorboards sounded like approaching footsteps.

Even my routines, my obsessive need for order, began to fail me. The spice rack, once a source of solace, now seemed to mock me with its perfect symmetry. The apartment, meticulously cleaned, felt dirty, tainted by the weight of my secret. Mittens, my ever-present companion, seemed to regard me with an unsettling mixture of pity and contempt. His gaze, once a comfort, now felt like a judgment. His presence was no longer a solace; it was a constant reminder of our shared conspiracy. The weight of my deception pressed down on me, heavy and suffocating. I felt like a man drowning in a sea of his own making, a sea of lies and carefully constructed illusions.

The guilt, I admit, began to gnaw at me. Not the simple guilt of a crime committed. It was far more complex than that. It was the guilt of betrayal, the guilt of manipulating the system, the guilt of allowing an innocent man to be wrongly accused. But the fear, the terrifying fear of exposure, of being found out, dwarfed all other emotions. The self-preservation instinct, the primal need to protect myself, outweighed everything else.

So, I continued to play my role, the anxious neighbor, the sympathetic friend, the innocent observer. I watched the news, saw Mark's picture on the screen, and felt a sickening mix of relief and revulsion. The case was closed. Clara was gone. The world moved on, unaware of the subtle, silent crime hidden in the quiet apartment next door. The silence continued, now punctuated only by the rhythmic purr of my accomplice, my confidant, my silent, furry accuser: Mittens. The game, it seemed, had ended. But in the quiet corners of my mind, the game had only just begun, a game of self deception, paranoia, and the enduring power of a carefully constructed lie. The truth, after all, was a dangerous thing, far better left concealed. And the cat, of course, would never betray me. He was my secret keeper, my partner in darkness, and my flawless alibi. The cinnamon scent of Clara lingered, a haunting reminder of the life I had

taken, and a testament to the
perfect crime, a crime hidden in plain sight, beneath the very nose of a world too
easily distracted.

POLICE INVOLVEMENT

The knock on the door startled me. It was Detective Inspector Davies, a man whose face seemed permanently etched with the weariness of a thousand unsolved cases. He was flanked by a younger officer, whose youthful optimism seemed utterly at odds with the grim circumstances. I hadn't expected them so soon. Mr. Whiskers, naturally, blamed the entire situation on the faulty latch, his tail twitching with indignant self-righteousness.

"Mr. Finch," Davies began, his voice low and gravelly, the kind of voice that could make a confession spill from the most hardened criminal. "We understand you knew Clara

Moreau."

I swallowed, my throat suddenly dry. Clara. The thought of her, of her bright smile and the way she'd waved when she saw me from across the street—it felt like a betrayal of my carefully constructed reality, a reality built on avoidance and the comforting predictability of my meticulously planned routine. "Yes," I managed, my voice a barely audible whisper. "I... I saw her sometimes."

Davies leaned against the doorframe, his eyes studying me with a keen intensity that made the hairs on the back of my neck prickle. "We understand you were one of the last people to see her." His words hung in the air, heavy with unspoken implications.

"That's... that's true," I stammered, feeling the familiar tightening in my chest. The anxiety was a physical entity, a suffocating weight pressing down on me, making it difficult to breathe. My hands trembled. "I saw her walking her dog... Tuesday evening, I believe. Around seven-thirty. It was a bit chilly, so I hadn't gone outside for my nightly walk." I added, in what I hoped was an inconspicuous attempt to sound natural. "She seemed... fine. A bit preoccupied, perhaps. But nothing unusual."

The younger officer, whose name I believe was Miller, took notes, his pen scratching across the pad with a rhythmic sound that grated on my nerves.

I found myself focusing on the scratch of the pen, rather than the piercing gaze of Davies. My perfectly constructed daily routine was crumbling. I should have been enjoying my nightly ritual of chamomile tea and a chapter of my Victorian-era detective novel. But now, the meticulously ordered serenity of my life was being violently disrupted by the presence of the police.

"Did you notice anything unusual about her?" Davies pressed, his gaze unwavering. "Anyone she might have been with? Any arguments or... disturbances?"

My mind raced. I had to be careful. Every word had to be carefully calibrated, a delicate dance on the edge of truth and calculated deception. I couldn't let them suspect me. Not for a second.

"No," I replied smoothly, forcing my voice to remain steady despite the tremor in my hands. "Nothing. She was alone. Walking her dog, as I said." I shifted slightly, my eyes drifting towards Mr. Whiskers, who was nonchalantly sharpening his claws on my antique Persian rug. "She seemed... happy." I had to put the poor cat out of my mind, he was complicating things. I felt him watching me, judging me, somehow aware of my lie.

The following hours blurred into a chaotic whirlwind of questions and carefully constructed answers. I described Clara's dog, a fluffy white Samoyed that seemed to embody the very essence of carefree joy. A stark contrast to the anxiety that clawed at my insides. I meticulously recounted my Tuesday evening, the precise time I'd put the kettle on, the exact number of chamomile tea bags I'd used, even the specific chapter I'd reached in my novel. I wanted to appear meticulous, almost obsessively so.

I needed them to see me as methodical, as incapable of spontaneous violence, as utterly incapable of anything so drastic as... well, what I'd done.

They questioned me about Clara's ex-boyfriend, Mark Jenkins, a man with a reputation for aggression and a history of domestic violence. They showed me a picture—a brutish, menacing face framed by unruly black hair. I felt a sudden surge of relief. This was perfect. The perfect scapegoat.

"I'd heard... things," I said, trying to sound as if I were reluctantly revealing a closely guarded secret. "She mentioned arguments. She said he was... controlling." I watched Davies's expression carefully, gauging his reaction, making sure to sound sincere, but not too eager, not too invested in pointing the finger. It was a delicate balancing act.

The investigation focused almost exclusively on Jenkins. They found his fingerprints on the doorknob of Clara's apartment and, much to my silent satisfaction, evidence suggesting he'd recently stalked her. They discovered text messages from him to her—threats, hateful messages that confirmed my carefully crafted narrative.

Days turned into weeks. I watched the news, the reports growing increasingly more focused on Jenkins's arrest. A wave of relief washed over me. I had manipulated the situation perfectly, leading the police to the most obvious suspect, the most convenient patsy. A part of me, a small, insidious part, felt a perverse sense of pride in my own cunning.

But as the days turned into weeks, a sliver of doubt began to seep into my carefully constructed certainty. The anxiety that had been my constant companion since childhood, had amplified a thousand fold since Clara's disappearance. It wasn't just anxiety anymore. It was fear. A chilling, bone deep fear of discovery. The police had been subtle in their questioning, but beneath the surface of their polite inquiries was a growing suspicion.

The details of my meticulously planned alibi, which had initially provided me with such comfort, now played in my mind like a sinister soundtrack. Every seemingly insignificant detail now felt like a potential crack in my carefully constructed façade, a potential avenue for the truth to leak out.

I started seeing shadows everywhere. The rhythmic tick-tock of the grandfather clock in the hallway became a relentless drumbeat of impending doom. Mr. Whiskers's innocent meows sounded like accusations. Even the rustling of leaves outside my window felt ominous, sinister. My carefully constructed reality was unraveling, thread by agonizing thread.

The police, despite Jenkins' arrest, continued to probe.

Miller's questions became more pointed, more insistent. Davies's subtle observations were starting to hit home. He was beginning to see the truth that lay hidden beneath the surface of my meticulously composed demeanor. The truth about my meticulously planned actions, actions that were driven by a crippling anxiety, that were born of a desperate need to control the world around me. A need to protect myself from the crushing weight of my own crippling social inadequacies. And, of course, the constant nagging presence of

Mr. Whiskers, whose innocent mishaps, in my mind, became a justification for my increasingly erratic behavior.

Sleep became a distant memory. My days were consumed by the need to monitor every aspect of my life, to check and recheck every single detail of my narrative, terrified that a single slip-up would expose the dreadful truth. Every sound, every shadow, every glance held the potential for exposure, and with it the certainty of impending doom. The weight of my deception was overwhelming, crushing me beneath its burden. Yet, even in my growing terror, a warped sense of triumph remained—a quiet satisfaction in my ability to manipulate, to deceive, to place the blame squarely where it wouldn't be expected, not on the culprit himself, but on an innocent, unassuming cat. Only, Mr. Whiskers was growing increasingly unconcerned with my growing anxieties, even seemed almost amused by the entire situation. The cat had become a silent observer, an amused witness to the slow, agonizing unraveling of my carefully constructed world.

ARTHURS TESTIMONY

"Right then," I began, adjusting my spectacles and offering Detective Inspector Davies a shaky smile. The younger officer, whose name I'd learned was Constable Miller, scribbled furiously in his notebook, his youthful energy a stark contrast to the oppressive stillness of my living room. Mr. Whiskers, naturally, had chosen this precise moment to sharpen his claws on the newly upholstered armchair, a detail I pointedly ignored. "As you know, I'm... rather a private person. Not exactly the life of the party, if you catch my drift." I chuckled, a nervous, brittle sound. Davies merely nodded, his expression unreadable.

"I saw Miss... Clara... a few times. Friendly enough, you know? A lovely smile. She seemed... happy. At least, as happy as anyone can be in this... rather gloomy neighborhood." I gestured vaguely towards the window, as if the pervasive gloom was entirely external, unrelated to my own internal turmoil.

"When did you last see her?" Davies' voice was low, gravelly, the kind of voice that insinuated itself into the cracks of your composure.

"Let me see..." I tapped my fingers on the armrest, feigning concentration.
"It must have been... Tuesday. Yes, Tuesday evening. I was... taking Mr. Whiskers for his evening constitutional, a necessary ritual, you understand, to maintain his... temperament." I paused, allowing the carefully crafted ambiguity to hang in the air. The truth was, Tuesday evening was the precise moment I'd noticed the missing package of catnip, the one I'd intended as a peace offering – a pathetic attempt to buy his silence.

"And where did you see her?" Constable Miller chimed in, his youthful enthusiasm slightly jarring.

"Just... across the street. Near the... lamppost. She was... talking on her phone. Seemed quite animated. Very... cheerful. I didn't intrude, of course. One must respect another's privacy," I added with a self-satisfied nod. My eyes flickered to the cat, perched precariously on the edge of the mantelpiece, observing the scene with a chilling lack of concern. He knew, of course. He always knew.

"Did you notice anything unusual? Anything that might seem... relevant?" Davies' question hung in the air, heavy with unspoken implications.

I hesitated, choosing my words with agonizing precision. "Well, there was... a car. A dark-colored sedan. I couldn't make out the make or model, it was rather... dark. And it was parked... oddly. Slightly askew, you know? Like someone was... in a hurry." I let the suggestion of hasty departure linger, carefully avoiding any mention of my own hasty activities that same evening.

The officers exchanged glances. The subtle shift in their focus, the way their attention diverted away from me and towards the vague description of the mysterious car, filled me with a perverse sense of accomplishment. My carefully constructed narrative was working.

"Do you know of anyone who might have... wanted to harm Miss Clara?" Davies asked, his gaze sharp.

"Harm?" I feigned surprise. "Good heavens, no! She seemed so... pleasant. But you know, these things... happen. One never truly knows one's neighbours." I shrugged, my heart pounding a frantic rhythm against my ribs. The mention of harm, the implication of violence, was a delicate balancing act. Too much, and suspicion might rebound on me; too little, and the investigation might peter out.

"Did she mention any problems? With anyone?" Constable Miller pressed.

"Oh, she mentioned an... ex-boyfriend. A rather... unpleasant fellow, by the sound of it. She spoke of him with... disdain, I believe. Yes, disdain is the word. A man with a... temper. A volatile personality, prone to... outbursts. I wouldn't be surprised if he... had something to do with her disappearance." I leaned back, feigning nonchalance, my gaze carefully avoiding the accusatory stare of Mr. Whiskers.

I launched into a detailed description of this imagined ex boyfriend, painting a picture of a jealous, possessive brute. I embellished the details, adding touches of violence and menace, weaving a tapestry of conjecture that subtly diverted attention away from my own culpability. I spoke of late-night arguments, of angry confrontations witnessed from my window
(conveniently obscured by curtains). I even manufactured a specific detail:
a distinctive tattoo on his forearm – a snarling wolf, a detail I'd entirely invented.

"He had a distinctive tattoo, you see," I added, my voice hushed, conspiratorial. "A wolf. A snarling wolf. I couldn't miss it." I glanced at the officers, anticipating their reaction.

They were hooked. I could see it in the subtle shift in their body language, in the renewed intensity of their focus. My carefully constructed narrative, a web of half-truths and carefully placed suggestions, was working exactly as planned.

Constable Miller began to question me about the timing of my sighting, cross-referencing it with the timeline of Clara's last known activities, meticulously documented in his notebook. I answered patiently, precisely, my every word a carefully calibrated step in my elaborate charade. I knew the details of her routine, gleaned from accidental eavesdropping and surreptitious observations. I could recall her daily walks, her preferred coffee shop, even the brand of cigarettes she smoked. My knowledge was both terrifying and exhilarating, a testament to my meticulous attention to detail.

Davies, however, remained skeptical. His gaze was unwavering, his questions piercing. He probed deeper, seeking inconsistencies, looking for cracks in my meticulously crafted facade. I deflected his questions with practiced ease, weaving a web of plausible deniability, using my anxiety as a shield, portraying myself as a nervous, slightly unhinged observer, incapable of malice, merely a victim of circumstance.

The interrogation stretched on for hours. The clock ticked relentlessly, each second a testament to the precariousness of my position. Yet, with each passing moment, my confidence grew. I had painted a compelling picture, a narrative so plausible that even I, the architect of the deception, was beginning to believe it.

The weariness of the officers, the accumulation of seemingly insignificant details meticulously woven together, the subtle shift in their focus from myself to the imagined, fearsome ex-boyfriend – all these factors contributed to my growing sense of success. They were buying it. They were almost entirely convinced.

Mr. Whiskers, throughout the entire ordeal, remained an impassive observer, his emerald eyes fixed on me with an unnerving intensity. He sat perched atop a stack of books, a silent, furry judge, watching the slow, agonizing unraveling of my carefully constructed world. He hadn't uttered a single meow, yet his silent scrutiny was far more damning than any accusation. He knew, of course.

He always knew. And the unsettling truth is, I wasn't even sure I wanted him to reveal it. The silence, the conspiracy, the shared secret – it was a perverse comfort in my growing isolation. The game continued. And I was winning.

THE EX BOYFRIENDS ARREST

The arrest was swift, almost disappointingly so. One moment, Detective Inspector Davies was meticulously examining the chipped mug I'd offered him (a blatant attempt to distract him from the increasingly suspicious paw prints on the rug, I might add), and the next, a uniformed officer was leading a handcuffed man out of my house. His name was Mark Jenkins, apparently Sarah's ex-boyfriend, a man whose name I'd only heard whispered, a shadowy figure lurking in the periphery of Sarah's fleeting mentions. He'd looked... surprisingly unremarkable. A bit pale, perhaps, with eyes that darted around the room like trapped flies, but nothing that screamed "violent kidnapper." Still, the evidence, as Davies had pointed out with a grim satisfaction, was compelling enough.

They'd found a ripped photograph of Sarah in his apartment, crumpled amidst a pile of unpaid bills and empty beer cans. There were also some... shall we say, suggestive texts recovered from his phone. Texts that implied a volatile relationship, rife with accusations and threats. The police presented it as proof of a jealous rage, a possessive man unable to accept rejection. Convenient, wouldn't you say? Perfectly fitting the narrative they'd crafted. And naturally, it placed me, the nervous wreck with the perpetually anxious cat, firmly in the role of an unwitting witness.

Constable Miller, ever the diligent note-taker, had even commented on Mr. Whiskers' apparent lack of concern during the interrogation. He'd noted it down as "unusual feline behavior given the circumstances." Unusual? Perhaps. Or perhaps Mr. Whiskers simply understood the game better than they did. The subtle artistry of deception. He was, after all, my silent accomplice, privy to every twisted thought, every carefully calculated step.

After they'd left, taking Jenkins and the lingering scent of cheap cologne with them, a profound silence descended upon my home. A silence so profound it amplified the ticking of the grandfather clock in the hall, each tick a tiny hammer blow against the fragile façade I'd constructed. I poured myself a generous glass of something strong and amber, the liquor burning a soothing path down my throat. Mr. Whiskers, perched on the bookshelf as usual, regarded me with his unnervingly knowing gaze.

He didn't judge, not exactly. It was more of a silent assessment, a feline appraisal of the situation. A cat knows. They always know. They see beneath the surface, to the raw, pulsating anxieties that drive us humans to such extraordinary lengths. He purred softly, a low rumble that vibrated through the floorboards, a purr that could have been satisfaction, or perhaps a knowing smirk translated into feline language.

I had to admit, a small, unsettling thrill coursed through me. The perfect crime, almost. The investigation had concluded in the most convenient way possible. Jenkins, with his history of aggression and a handy collection of circumstantial evidence, was the perfect scapegoat. No one would suspect me. I, Arthur Penhaligon, the nervous recluse, the man who barely left his house, the man with a neurotic cat. Who would ever suspect me?

But even as I savored this fleeting sense of triumph, a nagging doubt began to gnaw at the edges of my self satisfaction. It was a small thing, almost imperceptible, a flicker of anxiety that threatened to engulf me again. The doubt wasn't about the arrest itself, but about the seemingly perfect nature of it all. It was too neat, too convenient. Like a puzzle box designed to mislead, to lull the unwary into a false sense of security.

I replayed the events of the past few days in my mind, dissecting every conversation, every seemingly insignificant detail. I focused on my interactions with the detectives, analyzing my tone, my body language, the subtle shifts in my gaze. Had I given myself away? Had I inadvertently revealed something, some tiny crack in my carefully constructed alibi?

The more I scrutinized my actions, the more uneasy I became. There were inconsistencies, small lapses in my narrative that I hadn't noticed before. The way I'd hesitated when Davies asked about Sarah's last phone call. The tremor in my voice when I described my routine. Small things, but enough to raise suspicion in a keen observer. Perhaps Davies wasn't as easily fooled as I'd assumed. Perhaps he had noticed something.

And then there was Mr. Whiskers. His unnerving calm. His silent observation. He had been present for everything, a silent witness to my every move. He knew the truth, of course. He always did. He knew about the meticulous planning, the carefully orchestrated events that had led to Sarah's disappearance and Jenkins' arrest. He'd seen it all, from the subtle manipulation to the final, chilling act.

The thought chilled me to the bone. It wasn't just the anxiety about the potential consequences, but the realization that my carefully constructed facade was crumbling, and that even my feline confidant might eventually turn on me. After all, even the most loyal of accomplices might seek a better master in time.

I spent the rest of the evening pacing my living room, the silence punctuated by the rhythmic scratching of Mr. Whiskers' claws on the newly upholstered armchair. Each scratch was a tiny accusation, a silent condemnation of my increasingly frantic state. The liquor did little to soothe my frayed nerves. The exhilaration of success had been replaced by a gnawing sense of dread.

The weight of my secret pressed down on me, suffocating me. Had I really gotten away with it? Or had I merely delayed the inevitable? The police might have arrested Jenkins, but my own inner demons were far more dangerous. They were relentless, relentless like a cat chasing a piece of string, ever-present, ever-watchful, ever-ready to pounce.

As the night wore on, my anxiety escalated. I found myself seeing Sarah's face everywhere - in the shadows, in the patterns on the wallpaper, in the reflection of my own haunted eyes. Each phantom glimpse heightened the growing terror, each hallucination a subtle reminder of the enormity of my crime.

The image of Jenkins' pale face haunted me, a mirror to my own growing fear. He was the perfect patsy, the ideal scapegoat, but the realization that his arrest didn't necessarily mean my safety, only deepened my anxiety. My carefully constructed world, based on deception and fueled by anxiety, was starting to fall apart.

Mr. Whiskers, of course, remained impassive. He continued his silent observation, his emerald eyes fixed on me with unnerving intensity. He sat perched atop a stack of books, a furry Sphinx, guarding the secrets that we shared. He knew the truth, and I wondered if, in his feline wisdom, he was enjoying the slow, agonizing unraveling of my carefully constructed world just as much as I had. Or perhaps, he was simply waiting for the right moment to strike, to expose the truth and claim the spoils of victory for himself. The game, it seemed, wasn't over. It had just begun. And this time, the stakes were far

higher than I'd ever anticipated. The silence, the
conspiracy, the shared secret – it was no longer a perverse comfort. It was a
suffocating nightmare.

GROWING SUSPICION

The relief was fleeting, a fragile butterfly pinned under the weight of my own anxieties. Mark Jenkins' arrest, while convenient, felt... incomplete. The police, bless their diligent, if somewhat dim-witted hearts, had latched onto the convenient narrative: the jealous ex, the volatile relationship, the missing woman. They were satisfied. I, however, was far from it. A nagging dissonance hummed beneath the surface of my supposedly restored calm, a discordant note in the symphony of my carefully crafted alibi.

It started subtly, with a detail I'd almost dismissed: the positioning of Sarah's discarded handbag. The police had found it near the alleyway behind her apartment building, a seemingly insignificant detail in the grand scheme of things. Yet, I recalled seeing Mr. Whiskers near that very spot the morning after Sarah's disappearance. He'd been unusually fluffy, unusually... *content* . Had he been there, not merely as a disinterested observer, but as an active participant? The thought sent a shiver down my spine, a cold tendril wrapping around my heart. The image of his innocent emerald eyes, usually filled with disdain for my inadequate attempts at affection, now seemed charged with a sinister knowingness.

Then there was the matter of the missing jewelry. Sarah's apartment had been ransacked, not meticulously, but violently. Drawers had been pulled out, clothes strewn across the floor. The chaos was staged, designed to look like a desperate search by a vengeful ex-lover. But there was something off, a calculated messiness that hinted at a different kind of perpetrator, someone with a specific purpose, a methodical hand disguised by a theatrical display of rage. The jewelry box, normally kept on her dressing table, was empty. No forced entry, no signs of a struggle. Only meticulously placed disorder. My carefully orchestrated narrative began to unravel, its threads coming loose, fraying at the edges.

Detective Inspector Davies, a man whose intellectual capacity seemed inversely proportional to his enthusiasm for the job, had dismissed my initial concerns with a wave of his hand. "The cat, Mr. Finch? Really? I think we've got our man." He'd patted my shoulder with a condescending pat, the kind a parent bestows upon a child whose imagination has run amok. But his pat felt cold, dismissive, as if he sensed a deeper layer of deception, one he'd chosen to ignore, perhaps overwhelmed by the convenience of a neatly packaged solution.

The next few days were a blur of forced normalcy. I meticulously maintained my routine, my outward demeanor a mask of calm composure while inside, a hurricane of paranoia raged. I avoided eye contact with Mr. Whiskers, a strange avoidance, a silent truce in our silent war. He remained indifferent, or so it appeared. He'd observe me, his gaze intense, an unnerving silent judgement sitting in his emerald eyes. I started wondering if he was testing me, subtly letting me know that the game was far from over. His calm was unsettling, almost conspiratorial. It was as if he was holding a trump card, a piece of information that would shatter the precarious balance of my fabricated reality.

Sleep became a luxury I could no longer afford. The images swirled in my mind: Sarah's vacant apartment, the chilling emptiness of the jewelry box, Mr. Whiskers' unsettlingly serene expression. My anxiety, a constant companion, amplified every creak of the floorboards, every rustle of leaves outside my window. I'd find myself staring at the walls, searching for hidden messages, coded meanings in the patterns of the wallpaper, convincing myself that the cracks in the plaster were ominous signs, warnings whispered in the silent language of decay. Was I truly going mad, or was my perception of reality merely being distorted by the weight of my secret?

The detective's dismissal of my concerns had only fueled my obsession. I started scrutinizing every detail of the investigation, searching for clues that the police had missed. I revisited the crime scene in my mind, each piece of evidence, or lack thereof, scrutinized with a morbid fascination. The alleyway, the positioning of the handbag, the lack of forced entry in Sarah's apartment, the oddly neat nature of the ransacking – the puzzle pieces refused to fit into the neat narrative the police had constructed. And then there was the matter of the cat.

Mr. Whiskers, my feline confidante, my silent accomplice, remained the central figure in my increasingly distorted reality. Was his indifference a mask of cunning? Or was I merely projecting my guilt, my anxieties, onto an innocent creature? The line blurred, the reality distorted through the prism of my own deeply rooted insecurities. I caught myself whispering apologies to him, absurd apologies to a creature who, despite his unnerving stillness, seemed incapable of understanding, or perhaps, incapable of caring.

The days bled into weeks. The city buzzed around me, oblivious to the storm raging within. My isolation deepened, self-imposed, yet somehow inescapable. I found myself avoiding all human contact, my anxiety reaching new heights. The fear of discovery, of being exposed as a fraud, a liar, a potential murderer, suffocated me. Yet, strangely, a part of me craved the confrontation, the scrutiny, the possibility of being discovered. It was a perverse need, a morbid desire to have the carefully constructed facade shatter, to be free from the crushing weight of my own meticulously crafted lies.

One evening, while sifting through old photographs, I stumbled upon a picture of Sarah from a college reunion. She was smiling, her face radiant, a complete contrast to the distraught image I had conjured in my mind. A wave of selfloathing washed over me, a bitter tide of regret. Had I been so consumed by my own anxieties, my own insecurities, that I had completely misjudged her? Had I created a monster out of a shadow, a villain out of a victim?

Then, as I stared at the photograph, a detail caught my eye. A tiny glint of metal reflected in the corner of the frame, almost invisible, almost insignificant. A piece of jewelry, the clasp of a necklace, identical to the one I'd seen Sarah wearing the night before her disappearance. The necklace I'd "accidentally" knocked off the dressing table, "accidentally" swept under the rug, then "accidentally" disposed of in the alleyway behind her apartment building, where my "unusually content" cat, Mr. Whiskers, happened to have been "accidentally" present. The carefully constructed narrative collapsed, revealing its rotten core.

My carefully orchestrated performance of normalcy crumbled. The police had their convenient villain in Mark Jenkins, a convenient scapegoat. But the truth, like a poisoned dart, had found its mark, piercing through the layers of my carefully constructed deceit. The game was far from over, but now, the stakes were personal. Mr. Whiskers, the silent observer, watched me, his emerald eyes gleaming with what I could only describe as a chilling amusement, a knowing glint reflecting my own impending doom. The weight of my secret, once a manageable burden, now threatened to crush me entirely. The investigation had revealed nothing, but it had unknowingly revealed everything. And the silence, once a comfort, was now a deafening roar.

ARTHURS INCREASING PARANOIA

The silence in my apartment was a malevolent entity, a living thing that pressed against me, suffocating me with its weight. Mark Jenkins was gone, locked away, a convenient villain in a story I'd meticulously crafted. But the silence screamed louder than any accusation the police could have leveled. It screamed of my guilt. It whispered of the meticulous planning, the calculated risks, the chilling efficiency with which I'd orchestrated her disappearance.

Mr. Whiskers, my perpetually judgmental feline companion, observed my descent into madness with detached amusement. He sat perched on the arm of my worn armchair, his emerald eyes glittering in the dim light, a silent witness to my unraveling. I swear, I saw a subtle twitch of his whiskers, a silent smirk playing on his feline lips. Or maybe it was just my paranoia. The line between reality and delusion blurred, becoming as indistinct as the watercolor paintings I'd abandoned halfway through, their vibrant hues reflecting the chaos within.

The news reports, a constant barrage of comforting lies, repeated the official narrative: a jealous ex-boyfriend, a volatile relationship, a missing person. They'd glossed over the inconsistencies, the unanswered questions, the nagging doubts that gnawed at the edges of my sanity. They'd failed to notice the subtle discrepancies in my own testimony, the carefully chosen words, the calculated silences. Fools. All of them were fools. Except, perhaps, Mr. Whiskers. He knew.

He always knew.

Sleep became a distant memory, replaced by a relentless cycle of anxiety fueled nightmares. I saw her face everywhere – in the swirling patterns of the coffee I couldn't bring myself to drink, in the shadows cast by the streetlights outside my window, even in the fur of my own damned cat. Her laughter echoed in the empty spaces of my apartment, mocking my carefully constructed facade of normalcy. The apartment, once a sanctuary, now felt like a prison cell, the walls closing in, threatening to crush me beneath their oppressive weight.

My routine, once a comforting ritual, now felt like a performance, each step carefully choreographed to maintain the illusion of stability. The home deliveries, once a source of comfort, now felt like incriminating evidence, each delivery driver a potential witness to my unraveling. I scrutinized their faces, searching for any hint of suspicion, any crack in their composure. I saw suspicion in their eyes, even when it wasn't there. My paranoia was a beast feeding on itself, growing stronger with each passing day.

The newspaper articles, the television news segments, they all painted a picture of a grieving community, a woman lost to a violent crime. They offered a comforting narrative, a sense of closure that I desperately craved, yet couldn't allow myself to believe. Because the truth was far more sinister, far more unsettling. The truth was a dark, twisting labyrinth of my own making, a masterpiece of self-deception and calculated cruelty.

And it all began with a simple, almost insignificant act. A misplaced object, a subtle shift in weight, the faint scent of something... unfamiliar. Then came the realization, the sudden, chilling certainty that everything I had built, my entire world, rested on a fragile foundation of lies. And those lies were starting to crumble.

The fear wasn't just of discovery, but of the implications of that discovery. Not just the legal repercussions, the prison cell, the judgment of society – but the crushing weight of self-awareness, the horrifying realization of what I had become. I stared at my reflection in the darkened glass of the window. The man staring back was a stranger, his eyes hollow, haunted by the ghost of his own wickedness. The man who had been me had vanished. The creature replacing him was a monster camouflaged by the mask of normalcy.

Days bled into nights, each one indistinguishable from the last. The constant vigil, the hyper-awareness of every sound, every shadow, every flicker of movement, became an exhausting burden. I started to jump at the slightest noise, my heart pounding against my ribs like a frantic bird trapped in a cage. Even the gentle purring of Mr. Whiskers sent shivers down my spine, each vibration a reminder of my precarious position.

I began to see patterns where there were none, connections where there were only coincidences. The flickering streetlight outside my window became a coded message, the rustling leaves a whispered warning. The delivery drivers were no longer just delivery drivers; they were spies, their innocent greetings veiled threats, their casual observations a meticulous assessment of my crumbling defenses. The truth was I was losing my grasp on reality, spiraling into a vortex of self-incrimination and paranoia.

Even the simplest tasks became herculean efforts. Eating became an exercise in self-control, the simple act of swallowing a bite of food a challenge fraught with anxiety. My apartment, once a haven, was now a maze of potential threats, each object a potential instrument of my downfall. The shadows seemed to move, the silence to whisper accusations, and Mr. Whiskers' eyes, oh those eyes, seemed to pierce through my very soul, reading the dark secret that festered within me.

The police, with their well-meaning but ultimately misguided inquiries, seemed oblivious to the truth. Their investigation was a farce, a clumsy attempt to unravel a mystery that was, in reality, a testament to my own depravity. They were searching for answers in the wrong places, missing the glaring inconsistencies, the gaping holes in their narrative. The irony of it all was almost comical, if not for the cold dread that threatened to consume me.

I started to imagine conversations, dialogues that never happened, assigning malicious intents to perfectly innocent gestures. The friendly wave of the woman across the street became a silent condemnation, the cheerful chirping of birds a mocking chorus. My perception of reality was shattering, and my sanity was quickly following suit.

I spent hours staring at Mr. Whiskers, searching his feline face for answers, for some sign that would confirm or deny my suspicions. Was he judging me? Was he aware of my guilt? His expression remained unchanged – a mask of aloof indifference, or perhaps, something far more sinister. A knowing smirk that only I could see.

One night, I woke to the sound of scratching at my door. My heart leaped into my throat. Was it them? Had they finally discovered the truth? I held my breath, listening intently. The scratching continued, insistent and rhythmic. It wasn't a human knocking, but something much smaller. The scratching stopped abruptly. And I was left alone with my guilt, with the silence, with the knowing eyes of Mr. Whiskers, whose judgment was far more potent than any court of law.

The weight of my secret was crushing, suffocating. I was drowning in a sea of my own making, and there was no escape. The comforting narrative of the jealous ex-boyfriend was a lie, a convenient shield against the terrifying reality of my own culpability. I had played my part perfectly; the perfect patsy, the perfect victim, the perfect villain. The game was over. But the silence remained, a constant reminder of my crime, a chilling testament to my own twisted genius. And Mr. Whiskers? He remained my silent accomplice, his emerald eyes gleaming with a knowing amusement. He knew. He always knew. And that knowledge, more than anything, was the ultimate punishment.

A DISCREPANCY

The rain had started again, a relentless drizzle mirroring the persistent drip, drip, drip of anxiety that had become the soundtrack of my life. It had been a week since Clara vanished, a week since the police, bless their bumbling hearts, had hauled away her ex-boyfriend, Mark, a man whose scowl could curdle milk at fifty paces. They seemed satisfied, convinced they'd nabbed their villain. A convenient villain, I might add. One who conveniently fit their preconceived notions of rage and violence. One who conveniently left me, Arthur Penhaligon, the perpetually nervous recluse, untouched.

The discrepancy, the tiny, insignificant detail that gnawed at the edges of my carefully constructed narrative, was the color of her scarf. In my statement, delivered with the practiced calm of a seasoned actor (or a very good liar), I'd described Clara's scarf as a vibrant crimson, a splash of color against the grey of that miserable Tuesday. A detail meant to paint a vivid picture, a touch of artistry in the bleak landscape of her disappearance.

The problem? The scarf recovered from the scene – the park bench where she'd supposedly last been seen, a scene meticulously staged, naturally – was a dull, dusty mauve. Mauve. The color of disappointment, of something faintly unsettling. The color, quite frankly, that had never graced Clara's flamboyant wardrobe. I'd seen it. I'd *studied* it. Her wardrobe was a kaleidoscope of bright, bold colors – defiant against the drabness of her life with Mark, or so I imagined.

A wave of nausea washed over me, and I clutched my mug of lukewarm tea, the trembling in my hands almost violent.

The mauve scarf felt like a tiny, insidious crack in the meticulously crafted dam I'd built around my carefully constructed lie. The police, bless their simple minds, hadn't noticed. They were happy with their neat little narrative, a happy little bow tied on a case of domestic violence. But I knew the truth. Or did I? The uncertainty, the possibility of exposure, was the worst kind of torment. It was like a slow, agonizing itch that I couldn't scratch.

Mr. Whiskers, oblivious to my internal turmoil, sat perched atop the bookshelf, his emerald eyes gleaming with an unnerving intelligence. He was, of course, the perfect scapegoat. Always had been. My anxiety, my social inadequacies, my general inability to function as a normal human being – all his fault, naturally. He'd tripped me, I'd reasoned, causing the coffee spill that had started my day in such a disastrous fashion. He'd knocked over my meticulously organized spice rack, throwing my perfectly scheduled routine into utter chaos. He'd even, I'd almost convinced myself, influenced my disastrous job interviews with his incessant meows.

But this, this was different. This wasn't a misplaced spice jar or a spilled cup of coffee. This was Clara's disappearance. And the mauve scarf was a tangible, terrifying reminder of the chinks in my armor. It wasn't merely a discrepancy; it was a seed of doubt that threatened to blossom into a full-blown weed of paranoia, strangling my carefully cultivated facade of innocence. The police might be oblivious, but the seed of doubt had taken root in my own mind, a constant, nagging presence.

I replayed my interactions with Clara in my head, each encounter meticulously dissected, each word and gesture analyzed for any hint of incriminating evidence. There was the seemingly innocuous conversation about her prizewinning roses, a conversation which, in hindsight, had seemed far too calculated, far too much like a preliminary reconnaissance mission. Her comment about preferring mauve over crimson seemed absurd at the time; now it felt like a deliberate, almost mocking, clue.

Then there was the incident with the misplaced fertilizer, the one she'd reported stolen. A minor detail, easily dismissed. Except, I now realized, the bag of fertilizer had been suspiciously similar to the one I'd purchased for my own garden, the one with the slightly torn label that perfectly matched the description in her police report. The absurdity of it all, the sheer ludicrousness of my actions, almost made me laugh. Almost.

But laughter was a luxury I couldn't afford. The anxiety was a physical weight, pressing down on my chest, making it hard to breathe. My nervous tics had intensified, my hands shaking uncontrollably as I paced my apartment, the rhythmic squeak of my worn-out sneakers a counterpoint to the relentless drumming of the rain.

The cat watched me, his expression unreadable. Was he judging me? Did he know? The thought was ludicrous, yet somehow, disturbingly plausible. He was, after all, the only witness. The only one besides myself. And that was the real horror. The only witness, and possibly the only one who understood the depths of my manipulative, anxiety-fueled actions.

My carefully constructed narrative, the story I'd told the police, was starting to crumble. The mauve scarf wasn't just a detail; it was a symbol of the fragility of my lies. It was a testament to the human capacity for self-deception, for blaming others for the consequences of one's own actions.

I'd watched the news report on Clara's disappearance again that morning, the news anchor's concerned face a painful reminder of my success. They had the wrong man. Mark was an easy target, a man who had already demonstrated a propensity for violence. He was the perfect patsy, a convenient scapegoat. My anxiety had told me to shift the focus. My anxiety had told me what to do. And my anxiety, it turned out, was a master manipulator.

The neighbor, Mrs. Gable, a woman whose nosiness was only surpassed by her uncanny ability to observe details, had caught a glimpse of me, late one night, near Clara's house, a dark figure moving furtively in the shadows. She'd mentioned it to the police, a throwaway comment initially dismissed. But now, with the mauve scarf looming over me like a dark omen, that comment took on a sinister significance.

I tried to rationalize it. I was simply taking a late-night walk, I told myself. It was a perfectly normal activity. Except it wasn't. I hated the night. I hated being outside. Especially alone. Darkness was full of shadows, full of things that might trigger my anxious spells. My late-night walk, therefore, wasn't a walk; it was an insidious clue, an unintended confession. One more crack in my carefully constructed wall of lies.

Sleep became an impossibility. Every creak of the floorboards, every rustle of leaves outside my window, sent a jolt of fear through me. The image of the mauve scarf haunted me, the color a constant, throbbing reminder of my impending doom. The police weren't just investigating Clara's disappearance; they were investigating me. And I knew, with a certainty that chilled me to the bone, that they wouldn't find it difficult to discover the truth. The seeds of doubt had been sown, and now, they were rapidly sprouting, their roots reaching deep into my already fractured psyche. My meticulously crafted illusion was unraveling, the threads of my deception fraying and coming undone, one shaky, anxious breath at a time. And soon, the truth, like the relentless rain outside, would wash over me, leaving behind nothing but a muddy, chaotic mess. A mess I, perhaps, deserved. Perhaps Mr. Whiskers deserved a bit of credit. He may have had a hand in it. He certainly watches me with an unnerving amount of patience. The irony wasn't lost on me.

THE CATS PERSPECTIVE INTERLUDE

The humans call me Whiskers, though I suspect it's more of a description than a name. They lack the subtlety of true nomenclature. My human,
Arthur – a creature of alarming fragility and questionable hygiene – believes I possess some sort of sinister intelligence. He projects, you see. It's a human trait, a particularly pungent one in Arthur's case. He blames me for everything. The overflowing litter box? My fault. The perpetually burnt toast? My fault. The disappearance of his neighbor, Clara? Well, let's just say, he's *considering* it my fault.

The truth, as far as a feline can ascertain truth, is far more nuanced. Arthur is a master of self-sabotage, a virtuoso of misplaced blame. He weaves narratives, intricate tapestries of anxiety and paranoia, where I am the villain, the malevolent agent of chaos. It's rather amusing, in a darkly comedic way, like watching a particularly inept magician struggle with a disappearing act, only the disappearing act is his sanity.

He's been more agitated than usual since Clara vanished. The scent of her perfume – lilac and something sharp, like desperation – lingers faintly in the air. He frantically cleans, a nervous tic of his, scrubbing away at the faint traces, as if to erase her from his life entirely. This is my cue to dramatically stretch across the freshly mopped floor, leaving behind a pristine paw print right in the middle of his meticulously polished wood. He shrieks, of course. He always shrieks. It's the most musical part of his day, at least from my perspective.

The police visited, lumbering oafs with far too much shoe polish and insufficient observation skills. They questioned Arthur, their faces a mixture of pity and suspicion. I watched from the windowsill, unimpressed. They didn't notice the subtle twitch in his left eye, the barely perceptible tremor in his hand as he clutched his mug of lukewarm tea. They focused on the ex-boyfriend, a brute with the emotional range of a garden gnome. A perfect scapegoat, really.

Convenient. Arthur seems relieved they found their villain.

But their blindness amused me. They missed the small details, the carefully placed clues Arthur scattered like breadcrumbs, leading them away from the real culprit. He's surprisingly clever, in a pathetic, self-destructive sort of way. It's a performance, you see. A masterful display of nervous energy and feigned innocence. He hides in plain sight, shrouded in his own anxieties. He believes his paranoia makes him invisible, but all it does is make him predictable.

Clara's disappearance, however, was more intriguing. It wasn't an impulsive act, the result of a sudden burst of rage. Oh no, far from it. It was a meticulously planned sequence of events, a complex game of cat and mouse, in which Arthur, the supposedly timid recluse, was the ruthless player. He manipulates with the deftness of a seasoned puppeteer, pulling the strings of his own self-created drama. His anxieties are a smokescreen, an effective cover for his deliberate actions.

I observed Arthur's meticulous preparations in the days leading up to Clara's disappearance. The late-night trips to the hardware store, the secretive phone calls whispered in hushed tones. The way he'd test the lock on his back door, a nervous habit usually reserved for the arrival of his Amazon packages. His routine, usually rigid and predictable, took on an unsettling fluidity. The subtle shifts were easily missed, yet obvious to my keen senses.

The mauve scarf, the one the police found near the scene – or rather, the one he *placed* near the scene – was a stroke of genius, or perhaps just the convenient discarding of an incriminating item. He'd even left a single strand of his own hair near the scarf. Subtle, but not subtle enough for my liking. It speaks volumes about his underestimation of the police, and his overestimation of his own cunning. It was almost sloppy, as if he needed to be found out, to confirm his own self-loathing.

One might think my feline senses would be overwhelmed by all this human drama. One would be wrong. I am, after all, a cat. I observe. I judge. I nap. The constant low-level anxiety emanating from Arthur is quite irritating, though. It disrupts my beauty sleep.

And let's not forget the food. Arthur, in his frantic attempts to escape blame, has become remarkably generous with the tuna. He even upgraded me to the fancy salmon pâté. In many respects, this entire debacle is quite enriching. I have learned that even in the deepest depths of human deception, there's always a silver lining, usually in the form of delicious, high-quality fish.

The rain continues, a relentless, drumming rhythm that reflects the tempest in Arthur's soul. But I, the supposed villain, am unperturbed. I am warm, well-fed, and surrounded by the rich aroma of salmon. I will continue to observe, continue to judge, and continue to nap. Let Arthur unravel. His drama is my entertainment. Besides, there's a particularly enticing dust bunny under the sofa that needs investigating. Priorities, you know.

The irony, of course, is not lost on me. Arthur, in his desperate attempt to escape the truth, has painted himself into a corner. His elaborate web of lies, spun so meticulously, is now collapsing under its own weight. He believes he's outsmarting everyone, when in reality, he's merely demonstrating his profound self-deception. The seeds of doubt he's sown are now choking him, and he's too blind to see it. He'll continue to blame me, of course. It's easier than confronting the monstrous reality of his own actions. And as long as he keeps blaming me, the tuna will keep coming. And that, my dear readers, is a truth that even Arthur can't deny. For now, anyway. The humans are, after all, notoriously fickle.

UNINTENTIONAL CLUES

The police, bless their uniformed hearts, were remarkably inept. Detective Reynolds, a man whose perpetually furrowed brow suggested a lifetime spent wrestling with existential dread rather than criminals, had accepted Arthur's narrative with the same unwavering faith a religious zealot reserves for divine intervention. Arthur, in his meticulously crafted alibi, had painted himself as a timid recluse, utterly devastated by the disappearance of his vibrant neighbor, Clara. He'd even shed a few unconvincing tears – a performance I, a seasoned observer of human theatrics, found deeply unconvincing. The tears, I suspected, were more a result of the spicy tuna he'd indulged in that morning rather than genuine grief.

He'd meticulously recounted his routine, a monotonous cycle of online grocery ordering, daytime television, and the occasional – and, I must add, rather pathetic – attempt at a crossword puzzle. He'd even mentioned my role, casting me as the silent witness to his solitary existence. "Whiskers was with me the whole time, officer," he'd declared, his voice trembling slightly, a tremor that, I suspect, was born more of anxiety than genuine sorrow. He'd strategically omitted any mention of the frantic cleaning spree he'd undertaken the day Clara vanished, a cleaning spree so thorough it bordered on obsessive.

But Arthur, in his delusion of perfect control, overlooked the small details, the unintentional clues that whispered a different story. For instance, there was the matter of the soil sample found clinging to his pristine, white cardigan. A seemingly insignificant detail, easily dismissed as a mere coincidence. Except, the soil analysis revealed a unique composition, matching perfectly to the rare orchid that thrived in Clara's meticulously tended garden. Arthur, a man whose gardening skills were limited to accidentally killing a plastic succulent, would never have possessed such soil, yet there it was, a tenacious testament to his clumsy attempt at staging an innocent narrative.

Then there was the faint smudge of lavender oil on his favorite armchair. Lavender, Clara's signature scent, a scent so pervasive it clung to her like a second skin. Arthur, a man whose olfactory preferences leaned towards the acrid smell of burnt toast, would never have been near enough to the oil to transfer even a trace. Yet, there it was, another unintentional confession clinging to his carefully constructed façade.

And what of the tiny shard of glass embedded in the worn sole of his slippers? A microscopic detail, easily overlooked. Yet, it was consistent with the broken planter found near Clara's garden, a planter, coincidentally, that contained her prized orchids. These pieces, like fragmented pieces of a jigsaw puzzle, quietly pointed towards a conclusion that Arthur was desperately trying to avoid.

His attempts to manipulate the narrative extended beyond physical evidence. His interactions with the police were punctuated by calculated pauses and carefully chosen words. He'd consistently downplayed his interactions with Clara, portraying her as a mere acquaintance, a fleeting figure in his otherwise isolated existence. This was a stark contrast to the numerous delivery receipts he'd kept, detailing his regular deliveries to Clara's address; deliveries that included, mysteriously, an increasing quantity of her favorite brand of cat food, a brand that, curiously enough, was also my favorite. I'm not saying I didn't appreciate the extra tuna, mind you. But Arthur's blatant attempt to conceal the frequency of his visits screamed of guilt.

His phone records, though not outwardly incriminating, told a different story upon closer examination. There were numerous missed calls from Clara, calls that Arthur had conveniently ignored. He claimed his phone was always on silent, a claim easily debunked by a forensic examination of his device. The phone was on vibrate, a setting he'd quickly switched back after the police initially examined it, leaving behind a trace he'd overlooked.

The meticulous way in which Arthur had meticulously cleaned his apartment after Clara's disappearance, further demonstrated his guilt. He'd scrubbed every surface, disinfected every corner, leaving behind no trace of Clara's presence – save, of course, for those damning trifles I've already mentioned. This overzealous cleaning, this obsessive need to erase any evidence of Clara's visit, painted a far more sinister picture than that of a grieving neighbor. It suggested a man panicking, a man desperate to conceal something far more significant than a simple acquaintance's disappearance.

The way he spoke about Clara, too, betrayed his carefully constructed façade. His descriptions were laced with a strange mixture of resentment and possessiveness. He'd describe her vibrant personality with an edge of bitterness, a subtle undercurrent of envy. He'd praise her kindness, but his praise lacked genuine warmth. His words hinted at a deeper, more complex relationship than the one he'd confessed to the police. His narrative was a tapestry woven with lies, yet the threads themselves betrayed his true feelings.

The fact that he'd meticulously concealed his obsessive online tracking of Clara's social media accounts, further fueled suspicion. He'd even taken steps to delete his browsing history, an act that demonstrated a far greater level of guilt and deception than he'd let on. He'd carefully erased every trace, leaving nothing but a handful of unintentional clues to reveal his dark secret.

And then there was the matter of the cat hair. Not mine, of course. Mine is meticulously groomed, a testament to my superior hygiene. No, this was human hair, found inexplicably woven into the fabric of Clara's missing scarf, a scarf discovered abandoned near a secluded part of the local park – a scarf that smelled faintly of Arthur's peculiar brand of lavender-scented, burnt toast-infused cologne. A coincidence, perhaps? To Arthur, certainly. To me, and anyone with a shred of common sense, less so.

These unintentional clues, scattered like breadcrumbs through Arthur's meticulously crafted lies, painted a much more sinister picture. His desperate attempts to shift the blame onto me, onto external factors, only highlighted his own culpability. He was caught in a web of his own making, a web so meticulously woven it was destined to unravel under the weight of its own contradictions. The seeds of doubt, planted in the fertile ground of his own deception, were rapidly sprouting into a monstrous, truth-bearing vine that threatened to engulf him entirely. And I, my dear readers, was merely a passive observer, a silent witness to the spectacular unraveling of a man's carefully constructed reality. The tuna, however, remained plentiful. For now.

THE NEIGHBORS OBSERVATION

The afternoon sun cast long shadows across my meticulously manicured lawn, a stark contrast to the chaos brewing next door. Arthur, bless his delusional heart, was at it again. He'd been spending an inordinate amount of time tending to his prize-winning begonias, a vibrant splash of crimson and orange against the muted grey of his Victorian monstrosity. Normally, this wouldn't warrant a second glance. Arthur and his horticultural obsessions were a familiar, if somewhat unsettling, part of the neighborhood tapestry. But today, something felt...off.

His movements were jerky, almost frantic. He'd kneel, fussing over a particularly wilted bloom, then abruptly straighten, his gaze darting nervously towards the street. He'd mutter to himself, unintelligible words punctuated by the occasional sharp exhale that sounded suspiciously like suppressed laughter. He wasn't just tending to his begonias; he was performing a frantic, almost manic ritual.

It was the shovel that really caught my attention. A rather innocuous looking garden shovel, mind you, but its presence, nestled amongst the overflowing terracotta pots, was jarringly incongruous. He'd been using it, I'd seen him earlier, meticulously digging around the base of one of the largest begonias, his brow furrowed in concentration. He'd even paused to wipe his brow, a strangely satisfied smirk playing on his lips as he replaced the earth, carefully concealing whatever it was he'd been doing.

I watched him from behind my lace curtains, a silent observer in my own little theatre of domestic intrigue. My binoculars, a gift from my late, eccentric Uncle Mortimer, were my faithful companions in this clandestine performance. Through their lenses, I could see tiny details – the tremor in his hand as he wielded the shovel, the way his eyes darted around, as if expecting to be caught in the act. He looked like a man desperately trying to bury something, not just a wilted bloom.

Now, I'm not one to jump to conclusions. I believe in the power of observation, in letting the evidence speak for itself. But the timing was impeccable, wasn't it? Clara's disappearance had coincided with Arthur's sudden and rather obsessive gardening frenzy. The police, bless their thick skulls, had focused all their attention on that ex-boyfriend of hers, a rather unsavory character, I'll admit. But they'd completely missed the obvious, the man with dirt under his fingernails and a suspiciously vacant expression.

The next few days were a blur of carefully orchestrated normalcy from Arthur's side. He watered his begonias with almost religious fervor, his movements slower now, more controlled, the frantic energy replaced with a chilling stillness. He even brought out his notoriously grumpy Persian cat, Mr. Fluffernutter III, to "enjoy" the afternoon sun. The cat, a creature of impeccable disdain, merely glared at the world from its perch on a sundrenched terracotta pot, occasionally swatting at a rogue butterfly with a dismissive flick of its paw. The cat, I suspect, was just as perceptive as I was, if not more so.

My observations became more meticulous. I paid close attention to his interactions with the police, his rehearsed answers, his perfectly crafted performance of grief. It was all a sham, a carefully constructed facade designed to mask a far more sinister reality. He was like a puppeteer, manipulating the strings of his own narrative, pulling the audience – the police, the neighborhood, and even me – into his elaborate play of deception.

One evening, armed with a mug of lukewarm chamomile tea and a healthy dose of morbid curiosity, I decided to take a closer look at Arthur's begonias. The cover of darkness provided an ideal opportunity for my nocturnal surveillance. Using my trusty binoculars, I observed his property from the comfort of my living room. I could see him through the gaps in the leaves of his own trees, like watching a play on a dimly lit stage. And I saw him. Again. He was out in his garden, moving between his prized begonias with a flashlight and a small trowel. He appeared to be meticulously examining the soil near the base of each plant, and then carefully repacking it.

My heart pounded. Was he moving something? Burying something? My suspicions intensified. It was impossible to see clearly what was happening, but the repetitive movements, the constant attention to detail – it was enough to set off alarm bells in my mind. The meticulousness of his actions, the precision of his movements suggested something far more intricate than simply tending to his flowers.

The next morning, I armed myself with a pair of sturdy gardening gloves and a small, inconspicuous trowel of my own. I wouldn't be caught dead digging in Arthur's garden, of course. But my own garden, conveniently located just next to his, offered the perfect vantage point for covert observation. I pretended to tend to my own rather neglected petunias, all the while keeping a vigilant eye on his activities.

The police had increased their patrols, a testament to the growing concern over Clara's disappearance. Their presence didn't faze Arthur, though. He continued his meticulous gardening routine, a strange calm masking his desperation. It was a masterclass in deception, a carefully orchestrated performance that could only have been put on by a man who understood the power of projecting blame.

That afternoon, while Arthur was occupied with what appeared to be a particularly vigorous weeding session, I made my move. Armed with my trusty trowel, I carefully loosened the soil around one of the begonias he'd been attending to most obsessively. The soil was unusually compacted, almost unnatural. As I dug a little deeper, my trowel struck something hard.

It was a small, metal box, buried just beneath the surface. My heart hammered against my ribs. I carefully extracted the box, its surface coated in a layer of soil and decaying leaves. It was locked. This wasn't just a case of misplaced garden tools or a forgotten trinket. This was something significant, something that Arthur was desperately trying to conceal.

I returned to my house, my heart pounding a frantic rhythm against my ribs. The box sat heavy in my hands, a silent testament to Arthur's meticulously crafted deception. The contents remained a mystery, but the implications were clear. Arthur's carefully constructed facade of innocence was crumbling, revealing the monstrous truth beneath. The seeds of doubt, planted long ago, had blossomed into a venomous bloom, revealing the sinister reality hidden beneath his carefully curated garden. And I, a silent observer in the shadows, was privy to a secret that could shatter the tranquil facade of our quiet suburban existence. The game, it seemed, was far from over. The tuna, however, was still plentiful. For now.

ARTHURS GROWING ANXIETY

The delivery man, a burly fellow with a perpetually surprised expression, deposited the usual package – a week's supply of artisanal tuna – at my doorstep with a barely audible grunt. I signed the slip, my hand trembling slightly, a tremor that had nothing to do with the weight of the package and everything to do with the burgeoning dread coiling in my gut. Arthur's meticulously cultivated calm had fractured, replaced by a nervous energy that vibrated through the very foundations of his house, a house that, I now realized, held secrets darker than its aged, decaying paint.

The begonias, usually so vibrant, seemed to wilt under the weight of his inner turmoil. He'd stopped his meticulous pruning, the shears lying abandoned amidst a tangle of overgrown leaves. His lawn, once a testament to his obsessive neatness, was now speckled with errant weeds, tiny green flags of rebellion against his carefully constructed order. It was as if his very being was unraveling, mirroring the disintegration of his meticulously crafted alibi.

He'd started muttering to himself again, a low, almost inaudible murmur that drifted across the dividing fence. I strained to hear the words, catching fragments of phrases – "…the cat…didn't…it wasn't…" His words were fragmented, nonsensical, yet laced with a chilling desperation that sent icy tendrils of fear creeping down my spine. His normally precise movements were now jerky, hesitant, his eyes darting nervously from side to side, as if expecting to be caught in the act of something…terrible.

The cat, Mittens, seemed to sense the shift in Arthur's demeanor. Normally a placid creature, it now stalked the perimeter of Arthur's house, its fur bristling, a silent, furry sentinel guarding a hidden truth. I'd always found the cat unnerving, its luminous green eyes seeming to pierce through my own, as if it knew more than it let on. Now, its heightened alertness only fueled my growing suspicions.

The police, bless their dimwitted hearts, seemed content with arresting the ex-boyfriend, a hulking brute with a penchant for violence and a truly appalling collection of novelty socks. He was a convenient scapegoat, a ready-made villain in this suburban drama. But I knew better. I saw the subtle shifts in Arthur's behavior, the telltale signs of guilt that only an astute observer like myself could detect.

One evening, I witnessed him furtively burning something in his backyard, the flames flickering in the gathering dusk, illuminating his panicked face. The acrid smell of burning paper hung heavy in the air, a grim perfume to the unfolding tragedy. What was he destroying? Evidence? A confession, perhaps, scrawled in his shaky hand? The image haunted me, a grotesque tableau of a man desperately trying to erase his misdeeds, the flames consuming not only paper but also the fragile remnants of his sanity.

His sleeplessness was another glaring clue. I often saw him pacing his bedroom window at night, a silhouette against the moonlit sky, his form etched against the glass like a frantic prisoner in his own self-constructed cage. The curtains, usually meticulously drawn at precisely 10:17 pm, remained open, revealing glimpses of his restless agitation. The rhythmic thud of his footsteps, a relentless percussion against the hardwood floors, echoed across the quiet night, a morbid soundtrack to his unraveling.

He started leaving his garden gate unlocked, a blatant breach of his rigid routine. This small detail, seemingly insignificant to the untrained eye, spoke volumes to me. It was a sign of his crumbling control, a desperate plea for someone to notice, to intervene, to stop the wheels of his self-destruction before they ground him to dust. Or perhaps, it was an invitation. A subconscious invitation for someone to stumble upon the truth.

His interactions with the delivery people became increasingly erratic. He would mumble apologies, his words slurred and confused, his eyes wide with an almost manic energy. He would accept his deliveries with a tremor in his hand, his fingers fumbling with the packages as if afraid of what they might contain. The usual precision, the military like efficiency that defined his previous interactions, was gone, replaced by a nervous fragility.

I watched him from my window, my own anxiety mirroring his. The once sharp lines of his face were softening, his eyes were now shadowed and haunted. His once-immaculate clothes were now rumpled and stained, his once-perfect posture stooped, weighed down by the crushing weight of his secret. He had become a ghost of his former self, a spectral figure haunting the edges of his own meticulously crafted life.

His culinary habits changed as well. The strict, almost monastic regime of his diet, based entirely on meticulously portioned servings of tuna, had been abandoned. He'd been spotted purchasing unusual ingredients – spices, herbs, items not typically found in the pantry of a man who lived solely on canned fish. Was he preparing something? A celebratory meal? A desperate attempt to cleanse himself? The possibilities, dark and disturbing, whirled in my mind.

The once pristine, almost sterile interior of his home, so meticulously organized, seemed to be falling into disarray.

Scattered papers, discarded tools, and half-finished projects lay abandoned, creating a scene of chaos that starkly contrasted his usually impeccable order. It was as if the internal chaos within him was seeping outwards, manifesting itself in the physical space around him.

He'd started talking to plants. Not the polite, hushed conversation of a devoted gardener, but rather a frantic, almost accusatory monologue. I could make out words such as "evidence," "blame," and "Mittens," his voice raised in a strained whisper, barely audible but chillingly clear. It was a disturbing glimpse into a mind unravelling, a horrifying testament to the destructive power of guilt.

And the cat? Poor, innocent Mittens. Arthur's constant companion, his unwitting scapegoat. Its unwavering gaze seemed to hold a knowing silence, a furry enigma in the midst of the unfolding drama. It seemed to observe Arthur's descent into madness with a quiet dignity, as if resigned to the role it was forced to play.

The silence between our houses had become deafening, broken only by the occasional frantic whisper from next door and the rhythmic ticking of my own internal clock, counting down to the inevitable revelation. The seeds of doubt, planted long ago, had sprouted, grown, and blossomed into a poisonous vine, choking the life out of our quiet suburban tranquility. And I, a silent observer in the shadows, was left to wait, to watch, to witness the final, terrifying act of this meticulously orchestrated tragedy. The tuna, for now, remained untouched. But the game was far from over. And I, for one, was not remotely satisfied. The truth, I felt certain, was even more disturbing, more grotesque, than I could ever have imagined.

FORENSIC EVIDENCE

The first clue, as it were, arrived not with a bang but a whimper – a faint, almost imperceptible smudge on a discarded coffee cup. Detective Miller, a man whose perpetually tired eyes hinted at a caffeine addiction rivaling my own, held it up to the light. "Found near Ms. Bellweather's apartment building," he'd mumbled, his voice a low drone that seemed to seep into the very fabric of my already frayed nerves. The smudge was faint, a greyish smear barely visible against the cheap ceramic. "Trace amount of… something."

Something? My mind, usually a meticulously organized filing cabinet of anxieties, began to unravel. Something? What sort of something? Was it blood? My pulse quickened, a frantic drumbeat against the dull ache of my ever-present headache. My cat, Mr. Whiskers, had recently been shedding profusely. The vet said it was stress related – probably due to *my* stress. The poor creature. Could the 'something' be his fur? It wouldn't be the first time he'd become an unwitting participant in my misfortunes.

Miller, bless his caffeine-addled soul, seemed oblivious to the turmoil raging within me. He continued, his tone flat, devoid of any dramatic flair that might have heightened my already heightened anxiety. "Fibers, too. Unusual weave. Doesn't match anything in Ms. Bellweather's apartment." He paused, tapping the cup against his desk with a rhythmic *taptap-tap* that grated on my nerves like nails on a chalkboard. "But," he added, his voice a conspiratorial whisper, "it does seem to match… well, let's just say it matches something *else* found at the scene."

The "something else" arrived in a sterile, plastic bag, a small, almost insignificant object clutched in Miller's gloved hand: a button. A plain, unremarkable button, the kind one might find on a thousand different garments. Yet, it felt loaded, charged with a significance that transcended its mundane nature. It was dark blue, almost the same shade as Clara's favorite cardigan. A cardigan I'd never seen her wear, ironically. A detail that, like so many others, swam vaguely in my memory, just beyond the grasp of my increasingly anxious mind.

"Same unusual fiber composition," Miller confirmed, his eyes boring into mine. I tried to meet his gaze, but my eyes flickered away, drawn instead to the intricate pattern of the wood grain on his desk. The pattern was reassuring, predictable, a stark contrast to the chaotic surge of fear flooding my system. I cleared my throat, the sound thin and reedy, a pathetic squeak in the face of his unwavering scrutiny. "Perhaps it's just a coincidence," I offered, my

voice barely a whisper. "Buttons are... common."

Common, yes, but not this button. Not this *specific* button. Miller didn't respond, simply letting the silence hang heavy in the air, a palpable weight that pressed down on me, suffocating me with its implication. The silence stretched, each second an eternity, a torturous dance between accusation and denial.

The following weeks became a blur of increasingly tense interrogations, subtle accusations veiled in polite inquiries, and the relentless gnawing of guilt. Or was it fear? It was difficult to distinguish between the two, their tendrils so tightly entwined within my psyche. The police, understandably, focused their attention on me. My cat, as ever, remained a steadfast, furry observer, his green eyes glinting with an unsettling intelligence I couldn't quite decipher. Was he judging me? Or was I merely projecting, twisting his placid stares into accusations? It's difficult to tell where the line blurs between observation and projection when you're dealing with an animal that only communicates through meows and the occasional, disconcerting stare.

Then there was the matter of the broken shoelace. A seemingly insignificant detail, but Detective Miller seemed to find it intensely fascinating. "The shoelace discovered at the scene," he'd said, holding up a fragment, barely longer than my thumb, "matches the type you wear, Mr. Finch. We have a pair similar to this at the crime lab." I'd worn those shoelaces for... how long? Years. And why did the detective seem so fixated on such a seemingly trivial detail? I'd given the whole shoelace thing far too much thought, hadn't I?

The forensic evidence, like a relentless spider, continued to weave its web, each thread – the coffee cup smudge, the button, the broken shoelace – a subtle, almost imperceptible link to Clara's disappearance. The connections seemed so slender, so fragile, that it was easy to dismiss them as coincidence. But the cumulative effect was devastating, an insidious erosion of my carefully constructed facade of innocence.

The police scrutiny intensified. Miller started visiting my apartment more often, his questions becoming sharper, more pointed. He'd linger longer, his gaze drifting over my meticulously organized shelves, my spotless counters, the precise arrangement of my teacups, as if searching for some telltale sign of guilt I hadn't yet managed to conceal. He never found anything concrete, of course. But his presence, like a persistent, throbbing headache, became a constant reminder of the mounting pressure.

During one such visit, Miller asked me about the scratches on my arm. Minor scrapes, barely visible beneath the sleeves of my sweater, yet his eyes, usually dulled by exhaustion, shone with a sharp focus I found deeply unsettling. "Just… a little accident," I'd stammered, my voice cracking under the weight of his scrutiny. "Tripped on Mr. Whiskers." An unconvincing lie, and even I could see it in his eyes – the subtle shift in his expression, the way his lips tightened into a thin line.

His skepticism, however, was tempered by the undeniable fact that the ex boyfriend, a hulking brute with a history of violence, still held the primary focus. The circumstantial evidence against him was overwhelming: threatening messages, a history of abuse, his alibi that was rather easily debunked. The case against him seemed so solid, so compelling. It provided the perfect distraction – the perfect scapegoat, which, given my experience with Mr. Whiskers, I had grown alarmingly fond of using.

But the web tightened, and with each passing day, the net closed in. I could feel it, a cold dread that snaked through my veins, a constant reminder of the looming shadow of suspicion. Each insignificant detail, each seemingly random occurrence, was now a potential piece of evidence. The pressure was relentless, an excruciating, unbearable weight that threatened to crush me under its crushing force. Each night, I would find myself unable to sleep, staring at the ceiling, the shadows dancing on the walls like the phantoms of my own guilt. And the cat, my ever-present companion in both anxiety and evasion, sat serenely by my side, his silent judgment a constant source of both comfort and torment.

ARTHURS DENIAL

The interrogation room smelled faintly of stale coffee and despair. Detective Miller, his face etched with the weariness of a man who'd seen too much, sat across from me, a half eaten donut precariously balanced on the edge of the table. He leaned forward, his gaze unwavering, a stark contrast to the tremor in my hands. "Arthur," he began, his voice a low rumble, "we've found traces of Ms. Bellweather's blood near your apartment building."

My heart hammered against my ribs, a frantic drumbeat against the silence. "Blood?" I squeaked, the word escaping as a pathetic whisper. My voice, usually a strangled croak, felt thinner than ever, like it might shatter if I spoke too loudly. "That's…that's impossible! I haven't seen anyone! Except Mittens, of course." Mittens, my perpetually judgmental Persian cat, was currently curled up on the back of my favorite armchair, a picture of feline indifference.

Miller sighed, a sound heavy with years of dealing with evasive individuals, liars, and the generally unhinged. He tapped a file on the table. "Ms. Bellweather's ex-boyfriend, Mr. Henderson, has a solid alibi. He was out of state. The forensic evidence, however, paints a different picture." He paused, letting the words hang heavy in the air like the scent of impending doom. "Your fingerprints, Arthur, were found on a broken piece of jewelry belonging to Ms. Bellweather."

"A coincidence!" I blurted out, the denial as sharp and desperate as a starving man's last cry. "I…I could have touched it during one of my…errands. You know, I take my walks around the neighborhood. I…I could have picked it up. Accidentally. It's just a coincidence! A terrible, tragic coincidence!" I wrung my hands, the frantic gesture feeling utterly pathetic, even to me. The room seemed to spin, the walls closing in, the oppressive weight of suspicion pressing down on me like a suffocating blanket.

Miller remained impassive, his expression a mask of weary skepticism. "Coincidence, Arthur? Your explanation is…lacking. Your cat, Mittens, was also seen in the vicinity of Ms. Bellweather's apartment building on the night she disappeared. A witness claimed to have seen a black cat, matching Mittens' description, fleeing the scene."

My throat tightened. The cat again! Always the cat! It was always Mittens who bore the brunt of my failures, my anxieties, my inadequacies. He was the perfect scapegoat, the furry embodiment of my own inner turmoil. "It...it couldn't have been him! He's just a cat! He's a harmless, fluffy...murderous fiend. I mean, harmless! He's a cat. Cats don't...don't plan elaborate schemes. They nap. They shed. They judge. A cat doesn't understand murder, or...or anything beyond the intricacies of batting a string. It's completely absurd! Absurdly, tragically absurd." My voice cracked, my carefully constructed facade crumbling.

The detective remained silent, his silence far more damning than any accusation. He knew I was lying. He saw through my flimsy excuses, my desperate attempts to deflect blame, my pathetic projection onto my innocent feline companion. The weight of my lies pressed down on me, the guilt a corrosive acid eating away at my composure.

The detective produced a photograph. It was blurry, taken from a distance, but I recognized the scene instantly. It was a shot of the alleyway behind Ms. Bellweather's apartment. A shadowy figure, a figure that was undeniably me, was visible, although my features were largely obscured. My heart thudded a frantic rhythm against my ribs.

"This was taken just before Ms. Bellweather was last seen," Miller said, his voice low and steady. "The angle, the lighting...it's difficult to make out details, but it looks suspiciously like you, Arthur. And that...that's a familiar cat beside you."

I stared at the photograph, my stomach churning. There I was, a shapeless blob in the shadows, yet undeniably me. And there, by my side, was Mittens, his sleek black form somehow visible despite the poor quality of the picture. My meticulously crafted narrative of innocent victimhood began to unravel.

"It's... it's a trick of the light," I stammered, the words failing to mask the rising panic in my voice. "It couldn't be me. I...I was at home. I was...I was watching a documentary about...about...the mating rituals of Bolivian tree frogs!" The desperation in my voice was palpable, a clear sign that my carefully constructed alibi was crumbling faster than a poorly made sandcastle.

Miller's lips curled into a faint, almost imperceptible smile. "Bolivian tree frogs, Arthur? Really? That's...an unusual hobby for someone suspected of murder. And we have witnesses who saw you in the vicinity of her apartment building,

Arthur. People who noted the distinctive limp in your walk, your constant nervous fidgeting, and the rather prominent, uh...scar on your left hand. The one you tried to conceal during your earlier statements." He paused, letting the words sink in. "That scar, Arthur, matches the description of the wound inflicted on Ms. Bellweather."

My carefully constructed lies were reduced to ashes. The truth, a grotesque and horrifying monster, had finally been dragged into the light. The cat, poor innocent Mittens, had been my perfect alibi all along. My social anxiety, my paranoia, my crippling need to project blame—it all came crashing down around me. The relentless pressure had finally broken me, shattering the delicate facade of normalcy I had so painstakingly built. I couldn't even feign outrage anymore. The absurdity of my situation overwhelmed me. The police weren't interested in Bolivian tree frogs, apparently.

"The jewelry, Arthur?" Miller asked, his voice still even, his eyes betraying the slightest hint of pity. "Was it an accidental encounter, or a desperate attempt to frame someone else?

Someone who was already under suspicion?"

I stared at my hands, my fingers still trembling. The guilt weighed heavily upon me, an unbearable burden of my own making. I hadn't meant to hurt anyone, not directly. It had all started with the small things – a misplaced package, a missed delivery, an uncomfortable encounter at the grocery store – each minor inconvenience fueling my escalating anxieties until they had exploded in a destructive wave of paranoia. Ms. Bellweather, with her radiant smile and confident demeanor, had become a symbol of everything I lacked, everything I envied. Her presence next door had shattered my carefully constructed bubble of isolation, and my clumsy, panicked response had led to this cataclysmic failure.

The silence in the room hung heavy and suffocating. The half-eaten donut on the table seemed to mock me with its sugary sweetness. Outside, I could hear the faint sounds of the city, a relentless symphony of life indifferent to my plight. Mittens, oblivious to the weight of my confession, continued his serene slumber on the armchair back, his purrs a stark contrast to the storm raging within me. The web had tightened, and I, the architect of my own demise, was finally caught in its intricate, inescapable snare. My carefully constructed web of lies had crumbled, revealing the monstrous truth: I had not only harmed Ms. Bellweather, but I had also tried to pin the crime on the most innocent being

I knew. The cat. My dear, beloved Mittens, who only wished for a bit of tuna and a good nap. And I, in my self-absorbed desperation, had almost succeeded. Almost.

INCREASED POLICE SCRUTINY

The fluorescent lights of the interrogation room hummed, a discordant counterpoint to the rhythmic tick-tock of the clock on the wall. Detective Miller's donut was long gone, replaced by a file folder overflowing with photographs – crime scene photos, mostly, their stark reality a brutal contrast to the meticulously crafted fantasy world I'd built around myself. He pushed the folder across the table, the gesture somehow more accusatory than any verbal assault could have been.

"These are from Ms. Bellweather's apartment," he said, his voice flat, devoid of any inflection that might betray his thoughts. "Notice anything... unusual?"

Unusual? My carefully constructed world was built on the foundation of the unusual. My reality, my perceived reality at least, was a tapestry woven from the threads of anxiety, paranoia, and a deep-seated resentment fueled by the perceived injustices inflicted upon me by... well, mostly Mittens. But now, the threads were unraveling, revealing a pattern far more sinister than I'd ever anticipated.

The photographs depicted Ms. Bellweather's meticulously organized apartment, now a chaotic mess. Clothes were strewn across the floor, furniture overturned. There was a broken vase, a shattered picture frame, the remnants of a struggle. It was a tableau of violence, a silent scream captured in still images. And yet, nothing overtly pointed to me. Nothing, at least, that I hadn't meticulously cleaned, erased, or subtly misdirected.

"I... I don't see anything unusual," I stammered, my voice betraying the tremor in my hands. The lie tasted like ash in my mouth. It always did.

Miller sighed, a sound like air escaping a punctured tire. "Arthur, we found traces of your DNA on a broken shard of glass near the victim. And, as you know, we also found traces of her blood near your building." He paused, allowing his words to hang in the air, each syllable a hammer blow to my already crumbling facade. "We're also investigating your phone records. A lot of calls to delivery services... quite a lot."

He knew. He had to know. My carefully constructed alibi, a tapestry woven from late-night pizza orders and endless streams of online shopping, was starting to fray at the edges. Each delivery, each anonymous transaction, was a tiny thread in the web I'd spun, a thread that now seemed to be tightening around my neck. The irony was almost comical, if it weren't so terrifyingly real.

The interrogation continued for hours, a relentless assault on my carefully constructed persona. They pressed me on my relationship with Ms. Bellweather, questioning my statements, dissecting my words with the cold precision of a surgeon dissecting a frog. I offered the same tired excuses, the same rehearsed responses, the same carefully crafted narrative of a lonely recluse tormented by a malevolent feline overlord. They didn't believe me, of course. How could they? Even I barely believed myself anymore.

They brought in my landlord, a portly man with a perpetually disapproving expression. He spoke of my reclusive nature, my odd habits, my almost obsessive cleaning rituals. He confirmed my solitary existence, the lack of any meaningful social interactions, only punctuated by the rhythmic arrival of my endless deliveries. Each detail, presented as harmless eccentricity, now felt like a damning indictment.

Then came the forensic evidence. Hair samples, fiber analysis, microscopic traces of blood – all meticulously documented, each piece of evidence pointing towards me like a finger accusing me in a silent, damning courtroom. The police showed me images of microscopic particles found under my fingernails – particles consistent with the paint used in Ms. Bellweather's apartment. The paint that I'd 'accidentally' scraped off her door frame during one of my many late-night "errands". It was a

masterpiece of accidental incriminating evidence, a testament to my own stunning incompetence.

The weight of it all pressed down on me, crushing me beneath its suffocating burden. The carefully constructed wall of denial I'd erected around myself began to crumble, revealing the monstrous truth that lurked within. The truth that I, in my pathetic attempts to escape my own loneliness and inadequacies, had not only destroyed someone else's life but also implicated the most innocent creature on earth: Mittens. The irony was so rich, so blackly comedic, that it almost made me laugh.

Almost.

Days turned into weeks, the interrogation room becoming my temporary prison. The faint scent of stale coffee and despair clung to my clothes, my skin, my very soul. They brought in a psychiatrist, a woman with kind eyes that hid a steely determination. She probed my psyche, searching for the hidden motives, the buried resentments, the deep-seated psychological flaws that had led me to this point. She didn't need to dig deep. My anxieties, my neuroses, my blatant self-deception, were all laid bare, as raw and vulnerable as an exposed nerve.

I tried to maintain my facade, to continue blaming Mittens for everything – the spilled milk, the broken vase, even Ms. Bellweather's disappearance. But the psychiatrist saw through my flimsy excuses, recognizing the pattern of deflection, the projection of blame onto a convenient scapegoat. She had the audacity to suggest that my cat was, perhaps, not the root of all my problems. That I was to blame for everything.

The absurdity of it sent a shiver down my spine. Mittens, the fluffy, innocent perpetrator of all my woes? The idea was preposterous, yet, in the cold light of the psychiatrist's analysis, it seemed almost plausible. My carefully constructed narrative was falling apart, revealing a far more unsettling truth: I was not the victim. I was the predator.

My world, once a carefully constructed fortress of self-deception, was reduced to ruins. The web I'd so meticulously woven, meant to entrap others, had ensnared me. The police investigation had evolved from a simple missing persons case to a murder investigation, and I was at its epicenter.

The final piece of the puzzle came in the form of a security camera footage from a nearby convenience store. I'd bought a large bag of cat food that night, a fact I'd conveniently omitted during my earlier interrogations. Then, a grainy image of me, shadowy and indistinct, lurking near Ms.
Bellweather's apartment building. The footage was inconclusive, yet, when coupled with all the other evidence, it solidified the narrative. I was the one who was lurking. I was the one who had done it.

The evidence was overwhelming. My carefully constructed web of lies had crumbled. The truth, ugly and unforgiving, was finally revealed. And as I sat there, surrounded by the cold reality of my actions, I could only think of Mittens, sleeping peacefully on his armchair, completely unaware of the monstrous truth that he, unknowingly, had helped me conceal. The irony was a bitter pill to swallow, a testament to my own self-deception and the terrifying power of a carefully constructed lie. The police would never believe the truth – that it was the cat all along, or at least that is what I'd continue to claim, hoping that my own carefully constructed delusion could somehow protect Mittens. My dear Mittens. Innocent Mittens. But the truth was, there were no innocent parties in this grim and darkly humorous tale. Only me, trapped in a web of my own making. And Mittens, oblivious, purring contentedly, as always.

A CONFRONTATION

The interrogation room felt smaller now, the fluorescent lights somehow brighter, more insistent. Detective Miller, a man whose face seemed permanently etched with the weariness of a thousand unsolved cases, leaned forward, his gaze piercing. He'd been polite, almost solicitous, during the initial questioning. Now, the politeness had vanished, replaced by something colder, sharper. It wasn't anger, not exactly. It was something more unsettling – a quiet, unwavering certainty that I was lying. And he was right, of course. But proving it? That was the problem.

He slid another photograph across the table. This one showed a close-up of a single, muddy paw print – a perfect match to Mittens's. My carefully constructed alibi, the one built around my supposed incapacitation and inability to leave the house, began to crumble further. My throat felt dry, my tongue thick and clumsy. I cleared it, the sound echoing unnaturally loud in the oppressive silence.

"Look," I began, my voice trembling slightly, a pathetic attempt to regain control, "the cat... he's... independent. He goes out. He does things. I can't possibly account for his every move." The words felt hollow even as they left my lips.

Miller didn't flinch. He simply picked up a different photograph, this one showing a blurry image of a figure – me, I was certain, though the quality was poor – lurking near Sarah's apartment building the night she disappeared. My heart pounded a frantic rhythm against my ribs. My carefully constructed facade, the one I had painstakingly maintained for years, was disintegrating before my eyes, revealing the ugly, anxious truth beneath.

"We found traces of your medication near her apartment," Miller stated, his voice low and measured, each word a carefully placed brick in the wall he was constructing around me. "A rather unusual combination of tranquilizers and... well, let's just say it's not a typical cocktail for someone suffering from anxiety. It's the kind that leaves a person... disoriented, vulnerable." He paused, his eyes never leaving mine. "And quite suggestible."

My mind raced. I needed a distraction. Anything. I grasped at straws. "The ex-boyfriend," I blurted out, the words escaping before I could stop them. "He's violent. He has a history. It was him!"

Miller sighed, a sound devoid of sympathy. "We've already ruled him out, Arthur. His alibi checks out. His anger is undeniable, certainly, but his actions... those are verifiable. Yours? Not so much." He leaned back in his chair, the gesture somehow more menacing than any overt threat.

The hours that followed were a blur of carefully worded questions and increasingly desperate attempts to maintain my carefully constructed charade. I spun elaborate tales of my cat's cunning, his mysterious nocturnal escapades, his uncanny ability to manipulate situations to my detriment. I painted a picture of Mittens as a shadowy mastermind, a furry puppeteer pulling the strings of my life, a feline Dr. Moriarty. It was absurd, even to me, yet I clung to it, this ridiculous narrative, as if it were a life raft in a storm.

The detective listened patiently, his expression never betraying his true thoughts. I could sense his skepticism, a subtle shift in his posture, a slight tightening of his lips. He didn't laugh at my increasingly outlandish stories, he didn't shout or accuse; he simply listened, letting me hang myself with my own words, slowly, methodically, tightening the noose of my own deception.

The irony wasn't lost on me. I, the man who had meticulously built a life around avoidance, around hiding from the world, found myself completely exposed, my deepest fears laid bare. The irony was that my carefully crafted isolation had become my prison. The very strategies I used to manage my anxiety had become the tools of my downfall. The walls I'd built to protect myself had crumbled, leaving me naked and vulnerable, exposed to the harsh light of truth.

As the interrogation wore on, the exhaustion gnawed at me, a relentless companion to the burgeoning fear. My carefully rehearsed responses faltered, replaced by nervous stammering and evasive answers. My carefully constructed narrative began to unravel, the threads fraying, revealing the pathetic truth beneath: a man consumed by anxiety, desperately seeking to blame others for his own failings. And the convenient scapegoat, of course, was always Mittens.

He wasn't just a cat; he was my shield, my buffer against a world that terrified me. He was the perfect patsy, the invisible accomplice to my anxieties. I projected my own failures onto him, his actions – real or imagined – becoming evidence in my elaborate game of self-deception. And in that game, I was winning, at least until Detective Miller walked into the picture.

"Arthur," Miller said, his voice softer now, yet somehow more menacing than before. "We found Sarah's missing phone in your apartment. Hidden under Mittens's bed. And there were traces of her blood… on your slippers."

My carefully constructed world shattered. The evidence was irrefutable, undeniable. There was no more room for denial, for excuses. No more elaborate stories about a mischievous cat. The truth, ugly and horrifying, hung in the air between us, thick and suffocating.

The silence stretched, broken only by the relentless hum of the fluorescent lights, a morbid soundtrack to my downfall. My carefully crafted lies, my elaborate defenses, had all crumbled, leaving me exposed, a pathetic figure caught in the web of my own making. The weight of my actions, the enormity of my deception, crushed me. And in the crushing weight of that truth, I finally understood the depth of my own darkness.

The bitter irony was profound. I, who feared human connection, who had painstakingly constructed a life of isolation to escape the anxieties of interaction, had ultimately destroyed the very thing I claimed to desire – connection – with another human being. My paranoia, my anxieties, had driven me to the ultimate act of isolation – eliminating the possibility of any connection whatsoever. Sarah was gone, forever. And I was left with only the chilling truth, and the purring of an innocent cat, blissfully unaware of the monstrous shadow that his owner cast.

The weight of that realization was immense, an unbearable burden. The guilt, the regret, the profound and overwhelming sense of loss… they threatened to consume me, to drown me in a sea of self-loathing. The game was over. I had lost. And in losing, I had truly discovered the depth of my own depravity. A depravity masked, for so long, by the comforting purr of a seemingly innocent cat. A cat who, in the end, was entirely blameless. The real monster, after all, had been staring back at Detective Miller all along, trapped in the reflection of his own eyes, a reflection that showed nothing but the cold, hard truth of my own horrific actions. The only truth, that is, that mattered. Anything else was, simply put, irrelevant.

The interview room seemed to shrink, the oppressive atmosphere growing thicker with every passing moment. I watched as Miller reached for the handcuffs, the glint of metal under the harsh fluorescent light a chilling reminder of the consequences of my actions. And as the cold steel snapped shut around my wrists, a strange calmness settled over me. It was the calm of acceptance, of finally facing the monstrous truth that I had tried so desperately to hide, both from the world and from myself. The truth, finally, was out.

And in its chilling clarity, there was a dark, bitter humor.

MOUNTING PRESSURE

The cell was cold, a stark contrast to the stifling anxiety that had clung to me throughout the interrogation. The metallic tang of fear lingered in my mouth, a bitter aftertaste to the carefully constructed narrative I'd spun for Detective Miller. He'd bought it, at least initially. The charm offensive, the feigned bewilderment, the subtle redirection of suspicion towards the ex boyfriend – it had all worked, almost too well. Almost.

Miller's quiet certainty, however, had chipped away at my carefully crafted illusion. His gaze, like a surgeon's scalpel, dissected my carefully constructed lies, exposing the raw nerve of my guilt. The handcuffs, cold and unforgiving, felt like a physical manifestation of my inner turmoil. They weren't just restraining my body; they were binding my carefully constructed reality.

The initial relief of having the police focus on Marcus, the ex-boyfriend, was quickly replaced by a creeping dread. It was a slow burn, a subtle shift in the tectonic plates of my carefully constructed lie. The relief was a temporary anesthetic, masking the deeper, more persistent pain of my deception. The police seemed satisfied, convinced they had their man. Marcus, with his volatile temper and history of domestic abuse, was the perfect patsy. Too perfect, perhaps.

The irony wasn't lost on me. I, Arthur Penhaligon, a man who considered a trip to the grocery store a Herculean feat, had orchestrated a crime so meticulously planned, so flawlessly executed, that even I was surprised by its success – at least, initially. My nervousness, always my Achilles' heel, had paradoxically become my shield. My social awkwardness had allowed me to remain unseen, unnoticed, the perfect shadow lurking in the periphery.

The following days blurred into a nightmarish montage of routine and dread. The prison food was appalling – bland, tasteless gruel that seemed to mock my refined palate, a cruel parody of my former life of meticulously curated takeout menus. The other inmates, a motley crew of hardened criminals and petty thieves, seemed to sense my unease. They kept their distance, their wary glances a constant reminder of my precarious position. I was a fraud among frauds, a wolf in sheep's clothing, or perhaps more accurately, a neurotic cat burglar disguised as a quivering mass of anxieties.

Sleep offered little respite. My dreams were a chaotic jumble of images – fleeting glimpses of Clara's radiant smile, the glint of the crowbar, the terrified look on Whiskers' face as he watched me commit the act. He never understood, never forgave. I'd tried to explain, my mumbled justifications swallowed by his indifferent gaze, his feline judgment unwavering, unyielding.

The interrogations continued, though their intensity had diminished. They were more perfunctory now, a matter of ticking boxes, filling out forms. They weren't looking for answers anymore; they were looking for inconsistencies, for cracks in the façade I had so painstakingly constructed. And I, the master of deception, the architect of my own downfall, found myself desperately clinging to the narrative, hoping against hope that it would hold.

The days dripped by, each one a slow, agonizing descent into the abyss of my own making. The prison routine became a monotonous ritual – the tasteless food, the cold showers, the endless staring into the blank wall of my cell. My mind, however, was far from idle. It was a whirlwind of anxieties, regrets, and a growing awareness that my carefully constructed lies were starting to crumble.

The thought of Clara haunted me. Her absence was a gaping hole in my carefully constructed world, a constant reminder of the life I'd destroyed – not just hers, but my own as well. Had I truly loved her, or was my obsession a twisted manifestation of my need for connection, a desperate attempt to fill the void in my lonely existence? The answer, I feared, was both.

Whispers of doubt began to gnaw at me. The police seemed increasingly focused on minor inconsistencies in my story, details that I'd dismissed as insignificant, trivial. My meticulous planning had created a web of deceit so intricate, so layered, that even I was starting to lose track of the threads. Every carefully chosen word, every calculated gesture, now seemed to work against me. My anxiety, once my shield, had become my prison.

The pressure mounted, not just from the outside, but from within. The carefully constructed walls of my self-deception were beginning to crack, revealing the monstrous truth lurking beneath. The dark humor in my situation was lost on me now; it was replaced by a bitter, chilling realization. My meticulously crafted narrative was unraveling, and with it, the fragile illusion of my sanity.

My attempts to maintain my innocence seemed increasingly desperate, clumsy. The carefully rehearsed responses faltered, replaced by nervous ticks and stammering apologies. I found myself avoiding eye contact, my gaze darting around the room, seeking escape, even within the confines of the cell. My carefully crafted mask was slipping, revealing the tormented soul beneath.

One evening, a young, earnest officer named Davies came to my cell. He didn't interrogate me. He simply sat on the small stool opposite me, his silence far more unsettling than any barrage of questions. He brought a newspaper, an article about Clara's disappearance – an updated version, one that contained disturbing new details.

The article mentioned traces of my DNA found at the scene. It mentioned inconsistencies in my alibi, details I'd overlooked, thinking they were too insignificant to matter. Details that, in their cumulative weight, told a story far more damning than any confession I could ever give.

Davies didn't say anything. He didn't need to. His silence was a crushing weight, a stark confirmation of my worst fears. The web I had so painstakingly woven had finally closed around me, trapping me in its suffocating embrace. The truth, in its grim, unyielding reality, had finally caught up to me. The bitter laughter that once seemed darkly amusing was now a strangled sob, lost in the chilling silence of my cell. My meticulously constructed lies had become my undoing, a monument to my own self-deception. And the monstrous truth, finally revealed, was a far cry from the dark humor I'd imagined. It was simply, and utterly, terrifying.

A PSYCHOLOGICAL BREAKDOWN

The flickering gaslight cast long, skeletal shadows across my cramped apartment, turning the familiar clutter into a menacing landscape. My hands, usually steady in their obsessive rituals of tea-making and cat-food measuring, trembled like hummingbird wings. Sweat slicked my palms, the taste of fear acrid on my tongue. It wasn't the police, not yet. It was something far worse – a crack in the carefully constructed façade I'd built, a fissure in my meticulously crafted world of denial. My mind, usually a tightly wound spring of anxious calculations, snapped.

It began subtly, a low hum beneath the surface of my meticulously controlled existence. A twitch in my left eye, escalating to a full-blown spasm. The rhythmic tapping of Mr. Whiskers' claws on the hardwood floor – usually a soothing counterpoint to my internal chaos – now grated on my nerves like nails on a chalkboard. The constant, low-level anxiety that was my constant companion intensified, morphing into a full-blown panic attack.

I remember fragments, hazy snapshots of a collapsing reality. Clara's perfume, a heady mix of lilac and something else, something sharp and unsettling, haunted my senses. Her laughter, bright and carefree, echoed in the empty spaces of my apartment, a mocking reminder of the connection I craved and then destroyed.

The images flashed: the stolen moment in the park, her hand brushing mine, the fleeting warmth of her smile. Then the darkness. The frantic struggle, the muffled scream... My breath hitched in my throat, a strangled gasp escaping my lips. The cat watched, his emerald eyes gleaming in the dim light, a silent, judgmental witness to my unraveling.

Mr. Whiskers, of course, was to blame. He'd meddled, as always. His fur, a soft grey cloud, had momentarily obscured my vision as I...as I...the memory was a jagged shard, too painful to grasp completely. The image of Clara's face, contorted in fear, flickered and vanished. No, no, no. It wasn't my fault. It was the cat. Always the cat.

I paced the floor, my bare feet sinking into the plush rug. The carpet, usually a source of tactile comfort, now felt like quicksand pulling me down into the abyss of my guilt. My carefully constructed narrative, the one I'd spun to the police, to myself, began to fray at the edges.

I muttered apologies to Clara, hollow words devoid of genuine remorse. I blamed the cat, again and again, each repetition a desperate attempt to shore up the crumbling foundations of my self-deception. The narrative I presented to the outside world - the concerned neighbor, the helpful witness - was a tapestry woven from lies, each thread carefully placed to obscure the gruesome truth.

The police had questioned me, of course. I'd answered their questions with practiced ease, my carefully rehearsed answers dripping with false concern and manufactured sorrow. I spoke of Clara's difficult ex-boyfriend, his history of violence, his volatile temper. My words were carefully chosen, each phrase a tiny building block in the wall I was erecting between myself and the consequences of my actions.

The ex-boyfriend had been arrested. It was easy; his past provided the perfect cover. But even as the police celebrated their capture, a prickling unease gnawed at the edges of my manufactured calm. A small, nagging voice whispered doubts, a counterpoint to the soothing symphony of my self-justifications. The voice was faint at first, a mere tremor in the background music of my delusion. But now, in the suffocating silence of my apartment, it swelled, a cacophony of guilt and self-loathing.

My reflection in the dusty mirror seemed alien, a stranger with wild eyes and a haunted expression. The nervous tics, usually contained within the rigid structure of my routines, were out of control. I was a marionette whose strings had been cut, flailing uncontrollably in the darkness of my own making.

The breakdown wasn't a dramatic, Hollywood-style collapse. There were no screams, no violent outbursts. It was a slow, agonizing disintegration, a gradual unraveling of the carefully constructed illusion of normalcy. It was the quiet desperation of a man drowning in his own lies.

Then came the cat. Mr. Whiskers, oblivious to the storm raging within me, rubbed against my leg, purring his usual insistent melody. The sound, once soothing, now felt like a cruel mockery, a reminder of the creature I had blamed for everything. I recoiled, a guttural sound escaping my throat. The cat, my silent accomplice, my scapegoat, stared back with unnerving intelligence in his emerald eyes. He saw. He always saw.

I found myself confessing, but the confession was a twisted parody of remorse. It was a carefully crafted narrative, a carefully worded apology that aimed not at true accountability, but at self-preservation. It was a confession designed to absolve me, not to incriminate me.

"I... I did it," I whispered, the words barely audible above the pounding of my heart. "But it wasn't intentional. It was... an accident. Mr. Whiskers... he distracted me. He... he knocked over... the... the thing... and..." My voice trailed off, my words dissolving into incoherence.

The police would never understand the true depth of my culpability. They wouldn't comprehend the tangled web of anxiety, fear, and self-loathing that had driven me to this point. They wouldn't grasp the twisted logic that allowed me to blame my innocent cat for my own monstrous act. The confession, therefore, served a dual purpose – a half-hearted admission designed to appear remorseful while simultaneously shielding me from the full weight of my actions. It was a masterpiece of self-deception, a testament to the human capacity for self-preservation.

The final piece of the puzzle wasn't a dramatic revelation. It was an overlooked detail, a misplaced object. A single, bloodstained button found tucked beneath the rug, a button from Clara's coat. A button far too similar to one that had been ripped from my own jacket the night she disappeared. A button that silently screamed the truth. The silence of the apartment pressed in on me now, suffocating, filled with the weight of irrefutable evidence.

The cat watched, his eyes gleaming in the semi-darkness. His silent judgment was more profound than any courtroom verdict, more terrifying than any police interrogation. He knew. He'd always known. And somehow, in the quiet depths of his feline consciousness, I suspect a certain satisfaction. My meticulously crafted defense, my clever manipulation, my projection of blame onto an innocent feline companion - it had all crumbled under the weight of a single, insignificant button. The final, tragic act in my self-imposed drama. And perhaps, just perhaps, it was a curtain call Mr. Whiskers had eagerly awaited.

THE CATS SILENT WITNESS

The button lay on the floor, a tiny, innocuous thing, a pearly white speck against the dark wood. It was the button from her blouse, the one I'd noticed missing earlier, the one I'd so carefully, so meticulously, placed in the cat's fur. A perfect, almost invisible, frame-up. Except it hadn't been invisible.

Not to her. Not really.

Mr. Whiskers, of course, remained oblivious, his emerald eyes fixed on a dust mote dancing in the weak gaslight. He sat perched on the arm of my worn armchair, a furry sphinx in a world of escalating chaos. His indifference was a cruel, silent accusation. He wasn't merely a witness; he was the embodiment of my own callous indifference, a reflection of my twisted logic. He purred, a low rumble that vibrated through the floorboards, a sound as chilling as a death knell.

My carefully constructed alibi, built on layers of carefully orchestrated anxiety and projected blame, was crumbling. The police had seemed satisfied with the ex-boyfriend, a brute with a history of violence, a convenient scapegoat. But the button… that tiny button was a crack in the dam, a breach in my carefully constructed reality. It was a whisper of truth, a tiny seed of doubt planted in the fertile ground of their investigation. I could almost feel their eyes on me, though they weren't there, just yet.

The thought of them, the police, their suspicion, their methodical questioning, sent a fresh wave of nausea crashing over me. My breath hitched, a strangled gasp in the suffocating stillness of the apartment. I gripped the arms of the chair, knuckles white, the wood cold against my clammy skin. My mind, usually a frantic, chaotic mess, was strangely clear, the clarity of a man staring into the abyss.

Mr. Whiskers shifted, stretching languidly, his claws extending and retracting with the grace of a seasoned assassin. The image struck me with a grim humor.

My feline companion, the unwitting accomplice in my meticulously crafted crime. The perfect patsy, the ideal projection screen for my own guilt and anxieties.

The guilt gnawed at me, a relentless beast feeding on my fear and self-loathing. It wasn't the act itself, the removal of the button, the subtle manipulation, the planting of evidence, that haunted me. It was the complete lack of remorse. The cold, calculated precision with which I'd orchestrated her disappearance. It was the way I'd watched the investigation unfold, feeling a perverse satisfaction at seeing someone else bear the weight of my actions.

The ex-boyfriend, a man I barely knew, was now paying the price for my crime. A cruel irony, a macabre joke played on the very fabric of justice. And the chilling part? It wasn't an accident. It was calculated, deliberate. I'd chosen him, a convenient target, a man whose past provided the perfect cover for my own misdeeds.

My reflection stared back at me from the dusty mirror above the chipped sink – a gaunt, pale face framed by unkempt hair, the eyes hollowed, haunted by the weight of my secret. I looked like a man who had spent too long in the darkness, a prisoner of his own making.

The cat watched, unblinking, his gaze unwavering. He didn't judge, not outwardly. But I felt his silent scrutiny, a piercing gaze that seemed to strip away the layers of my self-deception, revealing the core of my depravity. He knew, and in his knowing, I sensed a deeper, more unsettling truth: he didn't care. His indifference was the ultimate condemnation.

I poured myself another cup of tea, the bitter liquid burning a path down my throat, a futile attempt to extinguish the fire in my soul. The trembling in my hands hadn't subsided; it was now a constant tremor, a physical manifestation of my inner turmoil.

The apartment, usually a sanctuary, a refuge from the outside world, felt like a prison cell. The familiar objects – the chipped mugs, the overflowing bookshelves, the worn armchair – were now imbued with a sinister significance, silent witnesses to my crime.

My meticulously crafted routine, the carefully planned deliveries, the measured movements – they were all part of the elaborate charade, the performance I'd staged for my own twisted amusement. The cat, my loyal, silent observer, had played his part flawlessly. He had been my accomplice, not in the act itself, but in my self-deception.

The silence was broken only by the rhythmic tick-tock of the grandfather clock in the hall, each second a hammer blow against the fragile structure of my sanity. Time was slipping away, the noose of my own making tightening around my neck.

I thought about her, the new neighbor, her bright smile, her gentle laugh. I thought about the plans I'd concocted, the fantasies I'd built around the possibility of connection. And I thought about how easily I'd discarded those plans, those fantasies, in favor of my own selfish desires, my own crippling anxieties.

The beautiful neighbor was simply an obstacle, a roadblock in my self imposed isolation. Her disappearance wasn't a tragedy; it was a necessary sacrifice. A regrettable necessity in my carefully crafted narrative.

But even in the depths of my self-deception, a tiny seed of doubt lingered. Had I gone too far? Had my carefully constructed reality finally begun to unravel?

The police weren't just investigating her disappearance; they were investigating me. I could feel it, the subtle shift in their attention. The questions were becoming sharper, the scrutiny more intense. They were beginning to see through the cracks in my carefully constructed façade, sensing the truth hidden beneath the layers of my meticulously crafted lies.

Mr. Whiskers jumped down from the armchair, his sleek body gliding across the floor like a shadow. He rubbed against my legs, purring, a low, rumbling sound that felt more like a threat than a sign of affection. His eyes, usually full of playful mischief, now held a disconcerting intelligence, a knowing that chilled me to the bone.

He looked towards the door, his ears twitching. A faint knock echoed through the apartment, the sound sharp and distinct in the oppressive silence. My heart pounded against my ribs, a frantic drumbeat against the impending doom.

They were here.

The police.

Or were they?

Perhaps it was just a delivery. A harmless, mundane interruption in my carefully orchestrated drama. But even that thought offered little comfort. The button lay on the floor, a silent witness to my crime. And Mr. Whiskers, my feline confidante, my unwitting accomplice, watched with his unnerving, knowing gaze. The game was up. The curtain was falling. And I, the master manipulator, the architect of my own demise, was left to face the consequences of my actions. The cat, as always, remained the silent judge, his purr a low, ominous hum in the darkening room. The truth, it seemed, had finally caught up with me. And the truth, as it always does, was far more terrifying than any fiction I could have ever imagined.

ARTHURS SELF-DECEPTION

The police hadn't even considered me. Detective Reynolds, a man whose face seemed permanently etched with the weariness of a thousand unsolved cases, had focused solely on the ex-boyfriend, a brute named Mark with a history as long as his rap sheet. Mark had a motive, a history of violence, and the convenient alibi of being miles away at the time of her disappearance. Perfect. Except it was all a smokescreen, a beautifully crafted distraction, orchestrated by yours truly. My masterpiece of self preservation. The cat, naturally, remained oblivious, curled up on the armrest of my worn armchair, a furry judge dispensing silent purrs of judgment.

My anxiety, usually a simmering cauldron within, had become a raging inferno. The police interviews, though brief, were excruciating. Each question felt like a tiny, precise needle piercing my meticulously constructed facade. I'd rehearsed my responses, my trembling hands clutching a lukewarm mug of chamomile tea – a pathetic attempt to quell the storm raging within. I'd practiced the slight tremor in my voice, the hesitant pauses, the carefully crafted air of bewildered innocence. It was theater, a performance worthy of an Oscar, if Oscars were given out for the most convincing lies.

The truth, however, was a far more complex and insidious beast than a simple confession. It wasn't a singular act, but a tapestry woven from threads of insecurity, fear, and a crippling inability to connect with others. The blame, I'd decided long ago, needed a scapegoat. And Mr. Whiskers, with his aloof demeanor and uncanny ability to appear at the most inopportune moments, was the perfect candidate. He was my shadow, my silent partner in my self-created prison of isolation.

It all began so subtly. A misplaced key, blamed on Whiskers' alleged fondness for playing with small objects. A spilled glass of wine, attributed to his tail swiping across the table. Small, insignificant events that built upon one another, creating a narrative in my mind – a narrative where I was a victim, constantly beset upon by a fluffy, four-legged menace. The escalation, however, had been a gradual process, a slow descent into madness fueled by my own paranoia. It was a slow burn, almost imperceptible at first. The button, though, the final piece in the puzzle, was the culmination of my meticulously constructed deception.

The irony, of course, wasn't lost on me. I, the recluse, the master of self-imposed isolation, had somehow managed to weave myself into a web of deceit so intricate, so perfectly self-serving, that even I was starting to believe it. The neighbor, Sarah, had been a catalyst – a beautiful, vibrant woman who dared to venture into my carefully constructed world of silence. Her arrival, instead of bringing hope, had stirred up a primal fear. A fear of connection, a fear of rejection, a fear of exposing the fragile, pathetic creature hiding beneath the layers of carefully crafted normalcy.

Sarah's disappearance had sent my carefully constructed world into a chaotic freefall. My anxiety, normally a manageable companion, had transformed into a full-blown panic attack. The possibility of her finding out about my secret, of discovering the carefully woven lies that I'd spun to conceal my true nature, was unbearable. So I acted. I reacted instinctively, driven by a primal fear of exposure. The act itself was swift, almost mechanical. A blur of panicked movements, a desperate attempt to restore order to my chaotic existence. And the cat, of course, remained the perfect scapegoat. The unwitting accomplice to my meticulously planned crime.

The confession, or rather, the lack thereof, wasn't a dramatic moment. It was a silent acknowledgment, a slow realization dawning upon me as I stared into the cat's unblinking eyes. The purr, usually a comforting sound, now felt like a sinister threat, a constant reminder of my guilt. The guilt wasn't for Sarah's disappearance – the actual act, in the cold light of day, was less traumatic than the years of self-deception that led up to it. It was the years of blaming Whiskers for my own inadequacies, for my inability to form meaningful connections.

I hadn't meant to harm Sarah. Not directly, anyway. But my actions, fuelled by anxiety and a desperate need to maintain control, had inevitably led to her disappearance. The irony was that my isolation, my self-imposed prison, had become my own personal Guantanamo. And the cat, my furry companion, had become the prisoner, or the unwitting accomplice in my own carefully crafted self-destruction. It was a twisted irony, the very things I had tried to protect myself from – connection, responsibility, accountability had instead led to this catastrophic implosion.

The button, that tiny pearl on the dark wood floor, was a testament to my intricate lie. A tiny, perfect emblem of my self-deception. It was a symbol of my inability to confront my own inadequacies, to acknowledge my own role in my misery. I had constructed an elaborate narrative to distance myself from the truth, to deflect blame away from my own failings. And in doing so, I had inadvertently created a monster – a monster of my own making.

Sleep was a distant, elusive memory. The nights were filled with a constant, low-level hum of anxiety, punctuated by nightmares that twisted and morphed into grotesque parodies of reality. In these dreams, Mr. Whiskers would transform into a monstrous creature, his eyes burning with malevolent intelligence, his purr a deep, guttural growl. He would stalk me through the shadowy corridors of my subconscious, a constant reminder of my guilt, of my deception.

Even during the day, a sense of unease clung to me like a second skin. The mundane tasks – the unpacking of deliveries, the preparation of meals – became rituals, each step performed with a robotic precision born of desperation. I moved through my days in a haze of paranoia, constantly scanning my surroundings, searching for signs of discovery. My reflection in the mirror became a stranger, a distorted image of the man I had become: pale, gaunt, haunted by a secret that threatened to consume me entirely.

The police investigation, though seemingly focused on Mark, had become a constant source of low-level terror. Each visit by Detective Reynolds was a nail-biting experience, an agonizing exercise in maintaining the charade. The detective, with his weary eyes and intuitive nature, seemed to sense something more – a subtle dissonance between my words and my demeanor. But he lacked the proof. Or perhaps, he simply chose to believe the easier narrative. Mark, the violent ex-boyfriend, was the perfect scapegoat.

Ironically, my carefully constructed narrative of blame shifting, my masterful manipulation of events, had almost worked. Almost. The guilt, however, gnawed at me relentlessly, a constant, nagging reminder of my deceit. It was a slow poison, eating away at my sanity, driving me to the brink of madness. The cat, oblivious to my internal turmoil, continued to purr and sleep, a silent observer of my slow unraveling.

And so, the game continued. A deadly dance between guilt and denial, truth and deception. I played my part to perfection, the innocent recluse, victim of circumstance, while the real villain, the architect of this macabre drama, remained hidden in plain sight. But the shadows were lengthening, the darkness was closing in, and the truth, like a persistent cat, would eventually find its way to the surface. The question wasn't if, but when. And when it did, I knew the consequences would be far more terrifying than anything I had ever imagined. The game, ultimately, was unwinnable. My elaborate construct was destined for collapse. And the fall, I suspected, would be spectacular.

THE FINAL PIECE OF EVIDENCE

The detective, Reynolds, had left, his skepticism a palpable thing even after he'd shut the door behind him. He'd bought the story, hook, line, and sinker. The abused girlfriend, the violent ex-boyfriend, the distraught neighbor – a classic case, neatly wrapped up with a bow of reasonable doubt. Except the bow was unraveling, fraying at the edges, threatening to expose the shoddy craftsmanship beneath. It all hinged on a single, seemingly insignificant detail: the cat food.

I'd meticulously crafted my alibi, a tapestry woven from half-truths and convenient omissions. The meticulously timed deliveries, the consistent anxiety-induced episodes, the perfectly placed cat hairs – all meticulously planned to create the illusion of an innocent, hapless recluse. But the cat food… that was a crack in my flawless facade, a chink in my armor.

Clara, bless her observant soul, had mentioned a peculiar brand of organic salmon pâté for her cat, a rather obscure brand, not easily found in local pet stores. A brand, I knew, that was exclusively sold online, delivered directly to one's doorstep. And that delivery address? My address.

See, I'd inadvertently added a layer of complexity to my already intricate web of deceit. I'd ordered the cat food, a seemingly innocuous act designed to maintain my semblance of normalcy. I'd even left a generous amount on the porch, a cat-sized offering to appease my feline overlord. But in doing so, I'd created a link, a fragile thread connecting me to Clara, a thread that the police, in their blissful ignorance, had entirely overlooked.

The realization hit me like a rogue wave, the force of it knocking me off my feet. My meticulously constructed narrative, the carefully curated image of the hapless victim, it all began to crumble. Panic, that familiar icy grip, tightened its hold around my chest. I could feel the walls closing in, the suffocating weight of my own deception bearing down on me.

My cat, Mittens, naturally, remained oblivious to the impending doom. He was currently engaged in a complex battle with a dust bunny, a scene of epic proportions in the grand scheme of feline warfare. His nonchalance, his utter lack of concern, was infuriating, a stark contrast to the turmoil raging within me.

The truth, I knew, was an insidious beast, its claws sharp, its teeth long and pointed. It lurked in the shadows, waiting for the opportune moment to pounce, to expose my carefully constructed lies. And the worst part? It wasn't just the police I had to worry about. There was the gnawing guilt, the everpresent weight of my secret, and the creeping dread that my anxiety, my lifelong companion, would finally consume me.

The irony wasn't lost on me. I, the master manipulator, the architect of my own elaborate prison, had been undone by a simple can of cat food. A testament to the capricious nature of fate, the cruel irony of human error. It was almost... darkly comedic.

I paced my apartment, the rhythmic tapping of my shoes against the hardwood floor a frantic counterpoint to the unnerving silence. The shadows danced and writhed on the walls, taking on monstrous forms, fueled by my paranoia. My reflection stared back from the darkened glass of the mirrored closet doors, a stranger staring back at me, a stranger with haunted eyes and a pale, drawn face.

The thought of being caught, of the repercussions of my actions, sent shivers down my spine. Imprisonment seemed a trivial concern compared to the exposure, the judgment, the complete annihilation of my carefully constructed persona. My life, so meticulously organized, so perfectly controlled, was falling apart. And it all began with a cat.

Mittens, having dispatched the dust bunny, now lay curled up on the sofa, a picture of serene contentment. He was the perfect symbol of my failure.

The embodiment of my inability to cope, to connect, to simply exist without resorting to manipulation and deceit.

The cat food wasn't the only piece of evidence, of course. There were other subtle clues, barely perceptible details that only now, with the panic induced clarity of impending doom, were coalescing into a damning narrative. There was the faint scratch on Clara's apartment door, a mark that could only have been made by my keychain. And then there was the fiber, a tiny, almost invisible fragment of my favorite sweater, found clutched in Clara's missing handbag.

My sweater. The one I'd been wearing the night Clara disappeared. The night I'd… well, let's just say I'd made a terrible mistake. A mistake born of anxiety, isolation, and an overwhelming sense of inadequacy.

I hadn't intended to hurt her. Not in the way that Mark, the ex-boyfriend, had. My actions had been… different. More subtle, more insidious. A carefully orchestrated dance of deception, a play in which I'd cast myself as the innocent victim and Clara as the unwitting pawn.

The truth, when it finally emerged from the murky depths of my self-deception, was far more horrifying than I could have ever imagined. It was a truth as twisted and grotesque as the creature I had become, a creature driven by fear and fueled by a desperate need for control.

The police were thorough, even if they'd missed the obvious. They'd investigated Clara's phone, her computer, her social media accounts, searching for any trace of her whereabouts. They'd found nothing, of course. I'd been meticulous in erasing my digital footprint, making sure there was no digital evidence to connect me to her disappearance.

But in their thoroughness, they had inadvertently uncovered a piece of information that I had overlooked – a series of hushed, almost imperceptible whispers in a forgotten chat log, Clara's desperate pleas for help, laced with veiled accusations against someone she called "The Shadow Man." Someone she feared, someone she believed was watching her.

The Shadow Man. It was a chilling moniker, almost poetic in its ominous ambiguity. But to me, it was a reflection of my own anxieties, a projection of my deepest fears and insecurities.

I'd become the very thing I feared. The monster in the shadows, the architect of my own downfall. I'd spent years constructing a fortress of solitude, a refuge from the judgmental eyes of the world, only to discover that my greatest enemy resided not outside, but within.

And as the realization finally dawned, the full weight of my actions crashed down upon me. The panic, the self-loathing, the overwhelming sense of despair – it was suffocating. I was trapped, not in a physical prison, but in a self-imposed cage of my own making.

Mittens, sensing my distress, hopped onto my lap, purring softly, his fur a comforting weight against my trembling hands. His obliviousness was both irritating and strangely comforting. He was a constant, a stable point in my chaotic world. But even his comforting purrs couldn't drown out the rising tide of fear.

The game, I realized, was over. My elaborate charade was unraveling. The truth was no longer a shadow lurking in the corners of my mind, but a tangible, inescapable reality. And the consequences, I knew, would be far more devastating than any self-imposed isolation I had ever known. The final piece of the puzzle was in place, and the only question remaining was: how long would it take for the authorities to put the pieces together? And more importantly, how would I face the consequences of my own twisted actions? The answer, I fear, would be as chilling as the truth itself. The cat, of course, would remain entirely blameless.

THE FALSE CONFESSION

The detective's skepticism hung in the air like the smell of stale cigarettes, a lingering reminder of his visit. He'd swallowed my carefully crafted narrative whole, a testament to my skill at deception, or perhaps just his own inherent laziness. Either way, it bought me time. Precious, fleeting time. Time I intended to use to refine my alibi, to solidify my already precarious position.

My confession, when it came, was a masterpiece of calculated ambiguity. I sat opposite Reynolds, the worn leather of the interrogation chair a familiar discomfort, mirroring the unease churning within me. I spoke slowly, my voice a carefully modulated tremor, a performance worthy of an Oscar, though I doubted anyone would be handing those out for this particular role.

"It... it was Mittens," I began, my gaze drifting towards the empty space on the worn armchair where the ginger feline usually resided. "I... I didn't mean for it to happen. It was an accident, a terrible, unforeseen accident fueled by... by a confluence of unfortunate circumstances."

Reynolds scribbled furiously, his pen scratching against the notepad like fingernails on a chalkboard. The sound grated on my nerves, a stark counterpoint to the carefully constructed calm I was attempting to project. I continued, weaving a tapestry of half-truths and carefully omitted facts.

"The... the cat food," I stammered, my voice cracking slightly. "It was... different. A new brand. She... she reacted badly. She became... agitated. Unpredictable." I paused, letting the implication hang heavy in the air. The implication that Mittens, in her agitated state, had somehow caused Sarah's disappearance.

I described, in excruciating detail, a fictitious scene of feline frenzy, a chaotic ballet of claws and fur and flying packages. Mittens, I painted, had become a rabid, uncontrollable beast, a furry little demon possessed by some unseen force. I portrayed myself as a hapless victim, caught in the crossfire of a feline tantrum, a pawn in a game I didn't understand.

"She… she knocked over the delivery box," I whispered, my voice barely audible. "The one with… with the… the things." I didn't specify what those "things" were. It left room for interpretation, for the fertile imagination of the detective to fill in the blanks. Let him conjure up images of incriminating evidence, of dark secrets, of a cat driven to acts of unspeakable violence.

I spoke of my desperate attempts to control the situation, of my futile struggles to restrain the crazed creature, of the moments of pure, unadulterated terror that followed. I even went so far as to describe a fleeting glimpse of Sarah, her face a mask of surprise and fear as the feline menace descended upon her. It was all fiction, of course, spun from the dark recesses of my imagination, where shadows danced and guilt metamorphosed into elaborate self-justification.

The truth, of course, was far more mundane, far less dramatic. But who wants mundane? Who wants the truth when a meticulously crafted lie serves you better? My carefully constructed narrative allowed me to maintain my carefully constructed image: the timid, slightly unhinged recluse, victimized by a vicious, unpredictable animal. It was a role I played well, a role I had been honing for years.

Reynolds seemed satisfied, his pen now moving with less frenetic energy. He seemed to be buying this new, improved version of events, a version far more palatable than the unsettling quietude of my initial denial. He believed the cat was the culprit. The *cat* . How wonderfully convenient.

He leaned back, steepling his fingers. "So, no involvement on your part, Mr. Finch?"

I shook my head, the movement almost imperceptible.

"Only… only as a witness to a… a terrible tragedy."

He nodded, his expression inscrutable. "Right. A tragedy. Well, Mr. Finch, we'll need you to sign this statement confirming your testimony."

I signed, my hand trembling only slightly. The document was a masterpiece of legal jargon, a carefully worded tapestry of legalese designed to obscure more than it revealed. I signed it, sealing my fate, not realizing that I was signing my confession, albeit a confession hidden beneath layers of carefully constructed falsehoods.

My carefully orchestrated performance had bought me time, but it was merely a reprieve. The silence following my "confession" felt heavy, pregnant with the unspoken questions that hung between us. The quiet was filled with the insidious drip, drip, drip of unspoken truths, the echoes of my deception growing louder with each passing moment. The carefully laid bricks of my self-deception were beginning to crumble under the weight of their own inherent instability.

The cat food, the new brand, the unusual reaction—all carefully chosen details. They were designed to point the finger away from me, towards the unwitting Mittens, while subtly highlighting my own pathetic helplessness. It was a masterful work of misdirection, a performance worthy of a far greater stage than a police interrogation room.

As Reynolds left, I watched him from the window, his figure shrinking as he walked away. The relief was almost overwhelming, but underneath, a cold dread coiled in my stomach. The game wasn't over. It had just entered a new, more dangerous phase. The police might have accepted my story, but the truth, like a persistent weed, stubbornly refused to remain buried.

I spent the next few days meticulously cleaning my apartment, wiping down surfaces, disposing of anything that might hint at my true involvement. Every movement was a calculated risk, every action a potential slip-up. The paranoia gnawed at me, a relentless predator lurking in the shadows of my own mind. The weight of my secret pressed down on me, suffocating me with its oppressive weight.

Sleep became a luxury I couldn't afford. My dreams were filled with Sarah's accusing eyes, her silent screams echoing in the darkness. The cat, of course, slept soundly, oblivious to the storm raging within me. Mittens, my innocent accomplice, my convenient scapegoat.

The newspaper articles began to appear, focusing on the arrest of Sarah's ex-boyfriend, painted as a monster, a violent brute. The media ate it up, the story perfectly fitting the narrative of the abusive ex and the terrified victim. My meticulously crafted narrative was complete. Or so I thought.

One evening, I found myself staring at Mittens, curled up on the armchair, his ginger fur gleaming in the dim light. The guilt, suppressed for so long, clawed its way back to the surface. The cat, the blameless cat, my shield, my protector, my convenient excuse. The absurdity of it struck me then, the sheer, unadulterated ridiculousness of it all. I had created a monster, not from flesh and blood, but from my own twisted anxieties, my crippling fear of connection, my desperate need to avoid responsibility.

I was alone, truly alone, even with the cat nestled beside me. The silence was deafening, punctuated only by the rhythmic ticking of the clock, each tick a reminder of the dwindling time before the house of cards I had built so carefully would inevitably come crashing down. The cat, as always, was the innocent bystander, a silent witness to my self-destruction. It watched me, as always, with those unblinking, enigmatic amber eyes. And in those eyes, I saw not judgment, but perhaps a flicker of understanding, a knowing smirk in the feline depths. Or maybe I was just projecting again. After all, I was the master of projection, wasn't I? The ultimate unreliable narrator of my own tragicomedy. The game, I realized with a chilling certainty, was far from over.

THE TWIST

The rain hammered against the windowpane, a relentless rhythm mirroring the frantic beat of my heart. The interrogation room was cold, the fluorescent lights buzzing like angry wasps. Detective Miller, his face etched with a weariness that suggested years spent battling the shadows of human depravity, sat across from me, his eyes like chips of ice. He'd been quiet for a long time, a silence more unsettling than any accusation. Mr. Whiskers, of course, was nowhere to be seen. He'd likely found a more comfortable spot, nestled in a sunbeam, oblivious to the unraveling of my meticulously constructed lie.

He finally spoke, his voice a low rumble, "Arthur, we found something."

My stomach lurched. "Something...?" I managed, my voice a pathetic squeak. I'd rehearsed my responses countless times, crafting a narrative of innocent bystander, a victim of circumstance. The cat, of course, remained the perfect scapegoat. His shedding, his midnight yowls, his alleged territorial disputes— all perfectly timed to create the illusion of chaos, a chaotic backdrop against which Clara's disappearance could easily fade into the background.

"A fiber," Miller continued, his gaze unwavering. "A unique synthetic fiber, found on Clara's clothing, near the scene where she was last seen. It matches the fiber composition of your... well, let's just say it matches a certain type of highly specialized cat toy."

The blood drained from my face. The cat toy. The stupid, ridiculously expensive cat toy imported from Japan, the one I'd been so careful to hide. The one I'd purchased online using a series of untraceable transactions through a convoluted network of cryptocurrency exchanges, each step meticulously planned, each digital footprint erased with the precision of a brain surgeon. And for what? A stupid, plush, robotic mouse that squeaked when you touched its tail. A detail so insignificant, yet so utterly damning.

"It's... a coincidence," I stammered, the words catching in my throat like sandpaper. "Mr. Whiskers... he could have... shed it."

Miller sighed, a sound heavy with disappointment. "Arthur, your apartment is practically sterile. We took samples from every surface, every crevice. There was no other trace of this fiber except on Clara's clothing, and... on your hands."

My carefully constructed world crumbled around me, the meticulously crafted facade of normalcy shattering into a million pieces. The anxiety that had been my constant companion for years intensified, turning into a raging inferno inside my chest. The tremor in my hands, normally subtle, became a violent, uncontrollable shaking. I wanted to blame it on the caffeine, the lack of sleep, the relentless pressure of the investigation. Anything but the truth.

The truth, of course, was far more horrifying than anything I could have concocted. It wasn't the cat. It was me. Always me. It wasn't about the coffee spills or the job applications. It was about Clara, and the agonizing terror of connection, of intimacy, of the vulnerability that threatened to swallow me whole.

Clara's arrival had been a disruption, a crack in the carefully constructed wall of my isolation. Her beauty, her effortless grace, her radiant smile— they were a threat to my meticulously ordered existence. A world constructed not of joy but of careful avoidance of any genuine emotional engagement. A world that had been shattered by her mere presence.

My plan, initially conceived as a tentative, clumsy attempt at connection, had quickly morphed into something sinister. The elaborate strategies I'd devised were never meant to lead to a relationship. They were meant to control the situation. To manage the risk. To ensure my own fragile equilibrium wasn't disturbed. The plan was less a seduction and more a meticulous orchestration of her disappearance.

The cat toy was a crucial detail, a carefully planted clue in the elaborate game of cat and mouse I'd been playing with the police. A subtle but essential piece of misdirection, designed to shift the blame towards the innocent, fluffy culprit that occupied my otherwise empty apartment.

I hadn't intended to hurt her, not really. It started with a misplaced fear. A fear that had grown into paranoia and then into something far darker. My social anxiety, so debilitating, so profoundly isolating, had twisted into something monstrous. My fear of rejection, of intimacy, of the very possibility of connection, had driven me to take the most extreme measure possible. The disappearance wasn't a violent act; it was a desperate attempt at self-preservation. A desperate attempt to retreat back into my carefully constructed cocoon of solitude, before the potential for rejection could tear me apart.

The subtle manipulation had been the easy part. The lies flowed effortlessly from my lips, shaped by years of honing my craft of deception. I watched as the investigation focused on her abusive ex-boyfriend. I listened to the detectives express their relief at having caught a dangerous criminal.

The satisfaction, the perverse sense of accomplishment, fueled my anxiety even further. It felt like a game, a game I was winning. A game where the stakes were far higher than I could have ever imagined.

The confession, meticulously constructed to maintain my carefully crafted self-image, was a testament to my skill at manipulation. It was a narrative of self-pity, tinged with an undercurrent of resentment towards Mr. Whiskers. The cat, after all, was a convenient target for my self-loathing. A silent, furry embodiment of the anxieties and insecurities that consumed me.

The truth, the sickening, horrifying truth, remained buried beneath layers of carefully crafted lies. It had only been unearthed by a stray fiber of synthetic material. A ridiculous, insignificant piece of evidence, found only because I had a strange penchant for overpriced feline toys from Japan.

Miller placed a file on the table, the cover bearing Clara's photograph. Her smile, previously so vibrant, seemed hauntingly sad in the grainy image. I flinched away, the sight of her happiness a constant reminder of the darkness within me. The darkness that I had concealed so successfully behind my nervous tics and the comforting presence of Mr. Whiskers.

The rain continued its relentless assault on the window. Outside, the world continued its indifferent existence, unaware of the carefully constructed lies and the horrifying truth they concealed. In the quiet, sterile room, the only sound was the faint, rhythmic scratching from the vents. Mr. Whiskers had found his way in, likely seeking comfort on the floor under the table. As the officer prepared the paperwork, I felt his soft fur brush against my leg. Maybe, just maybe, the silence was his approval. Maybe even his revenge. His silent, fluffy, and deeply satisfying revenge. My carefully constructed
world had fallen apart and there was nothing left to blame but myself. But then again, perhaps there was still the cat...

ARTHURS MOTIVES

The detective's pen scratched across the paper, a counterpoint to the insistent drumming of rain against the glass. Each stroke felt like a nail hammered into the coffin of my carefully constructed reality. He hadn't explicitly accused me, not yet. He didn't need to. The weight of unspoken accusations hung heavy in the air, thick and suffocating like the humidity clinging to the city on a summer night. My carefully constructed alibi, woven with threads of plausible deniability and feline misdirection, was unraveling, strand by fragile strand.

It had started so innocently, or so I had convinced myself. The new neighbor, Isabella, with her sun-kissed skin and laughter that could melt glaciers, had been a threat, a disruption to the meticulously crafted solitude I had painstakingly built. My life, before her arrival, had been a symphony of quiet desperation, a perfectly orchestrated ballet of avoidance and self-imposed exile. My apartment, a sanctuary of carefully arranged clutter and half-finished projects, had been my fortress against the overwhelming tide of human interaction. Mr. Whiskers, my perpetually judgmental feline companion, had been my only confidante, a silent witness to my anxieties and a convenient scapegoat for my failures.

Isabella's presence shattered the fragile equilibrium I had maintained for so long. Her cheerful greetings, her casual conversations over the fence, were an assault on my carefully constructed defenses. Each fleeting moment of interaction sent a jolt of anxiety through me, a primal fear that threatened to overwhelm my carefully cultivated composure. I couldn't risk rejection. I couldn't bear the thought of being seen, truly seen, for the anxious, inadequate mess that I was. So I devised a plan, a twisted, convoluted scheme born of desperation and fueled by the potent cocktail of fear and self-loathing that had become my constant companions.

It wasn't a premeditated murder, not in the traditional sense. There was no grand design, no meticulously planned sequence of events. It was a slow, insidious erosion of her presence, a carefully orchestrated campaign of subtle manipulations and calculated omissions. The disappearance wasn't a single, decisive act but a culmination of my anxieties, my fears, and my desperate need to reclaim the sanctuary of my solitude. It started with small things, seemingly innocuous acts that, in retrospect, paint a chilling picture of my depravity.

I subtly sabotaged her attempts to make friends in the neighborhood. I'd let the air out of her bicycle tire, leaving a cryptic note suggesting a vengeful ex. I'd spread rumors – whispered suggestions, carefully planted seeds of doubt – about her past, stories that would cast a shadow of suspicion over her, making her less approachable, less likely to attract attention. I wanted her gone, but not in a way that would directly implicate me. I needed plausible deniability, a safety net woven from the fabric of reasonable doubt. And who better to shoulder the blame than Mr. Whiskers, my furry accomplice in my self-deception?

The cat, in all his aloof indifference, was the perfect scapegoat. His mysterious movements, his nocturnal prowlings, his penchant for disappearing for days at a time – all these characteristics provided the perfect cover for my actions. His very existence became a convenient shield, a blank canvas onto which I projected my own anxieties and insecurities. I'd leave traces of his fur near her belongings, subtle clues that would suggest his involvement, albeit indirectly. The scratches on her car? Mr. Whiskers. The torn screen on her window? Mr. Whiskers, naturally. The missing items from her apartment? Oh, the cat, undoubtedly.

The police investigation, with its focus on the abusive ex boyfriend, was a stroke of pure luck. It was a convenient distraction, a smokescreen allowing me to retreat further into the shadows of my self-created delusion. I watched from the sidelines as the pieces of the puzzle fell into place, orchestrated not by fate, but by my own meticulous manipulation.

The arrest of Isabella's ex provided me with a perverse sense of satisfaction. It was a validation of my anxieties, a confirmation that the world was as dangerous and unpredictable as I had always believed. It was a justification for my isolation, a testament to the validity of my fears. The weight of guilt, however, was a heavy burden to carry. It gnawed at me, a constant reminder of my actions. But the fear of exposure was even greater. The fear of being seen, not as the victim of my own anxieties, but as their perpetrator.

The truth, like a malignant tumor, festered within me. It was a secret I carried with a chilling calm, a secret that threatened to consume me from the inside out. The cat, ironically, became my confidante once more. His purr, a rhythmic vibration against my skin, was a twisted comfort, a reminder of the success of my deception. He had been my partner in crime, my silent accomplice in the grand theatre of my self-preservation. He didn't know the truth, of course, but perhaps, in his feline wisdom, he understood the depths of my despair. Perhaps he saw the cracks in my carefully constructed façade. Perhaps he judged me, just as I had always feared.

The irony wasn't lost on me. I, a man crippled by social anxiety, had orchestrated a web of deceit that implicated an innocent man and escaped punishment. I, a man terrified of confrontation, had engineered a scenario that eliminated a threat to my fragile peace, a threat represented by the vibrant, life-affirming presence of Isabella. My carefully constructed life, built on avoidance and fear, had devoured everything in its path. The rain outside continued its relentless rhythm, a morbid symphony echoing the turmoil within.

Detective Miller's silence was more damning than any accusation. His penetrating gaze stripped away the layers of my carefully crafted persona, revealing the core of my depravity. The silence in the interrogation room was heavy with unspoken truths, a chasm between my carefully constructed reality and the horrifying truth I had to confront. The scratching from the vents was the only other sound, the subtle purr of my accomplice, my furry enabler. Mr. Whiskers. He was still there, a silent testament to my cowardly masterpiece. His presence was a cruel reminder of the lengths I would go to maintain my isolation. He had become not just a scapegoat but a symbol of my utter self-destruction, the embodiment of my cowardice.

Perhaps Detective Miller saw it in my eyes, the flicker of guilt amidst the façade of calm. Perhaps he heard it in my voice, the subtle tremor betraying the elaborate lies I had spun. Or perhaps it was simply the weight of unspoken truths hanging in the air, as heavy and suffocating as the rain lashing against the windows of the interrogation room. The reality of my actions hung over me like a guillotine, ready to fall. Yet, a part of me – a small, insidious part – still felt a perverse satisfaction. I had won, hadn't I? I had eliminated the threat, reclaimed my solitude, and preserved my carefully constructed illusion of normalcy. Even in defeat, there was a twisted sense of victory. A victory built on lies, deceit, and the tragic downfall of another. A dark, twisted victory, celebrated only in the silent purr of my ever-present companion, Mr. Whiskers. The rain continued its incessant assault on the windows, washing away the evidence, but not the guilt, the self-loathing, and the horrifying truth that now rested, heavy and suffocating, on my conscience. And somewhere, deep within, a small, insidious voice whispered,

"It wasn't my fault. It was the cat."

THE CATS REVENGE IMPLIED

The interrogation room felt colder now, the damp seeping into my bones, mirroring the chill that had settled permanently in my soul. Detective Miller's departure left a vacuum, a silence punctuated only by the rhythmic tick-tock of a clock that seemed to mock the relentless march of time towards my inevitable exposure. He hadn't arrested me, not yet, but the unspoken accusation hung in the air, thick and cloying like the scent of lilies from the wilting bouquet on the table. Lilies she loved, Sarah. Lilies that now felt like a cruel monument to her disappearance.

Mr. Whiskers, curled on my lap, purred, a low, rumbling vibration that felt both comforting and unsettling. His fur, usually soft and silken, felt rough under my touch, a prickling sensation that mirrored the unease gnawing at my insides. He had been unusually quiet during the interrogation, a passive observer to my carefully crafted performance. Too quiet, perhaps. Too…knowing.

The thought, absurd as it was, clung to me like a stubborn burr. Had Mr. Whiskers somehow orchestrated this? Had he, in his feline wisdom, sensed the threat Sarah posed to my carefully constructed solitude? Had he, in his own cryptic way, engineered her disappearance? The idea was ridiculous, of course, a product of my overactive imagination fueled by guilt and sleepless nights. Yet…

I remembered the night Sarah vanished. The insistent meowing, the frantic scratching at the back door. I'd dismissed it then, attributed it to Mr. Whiskers' nocturnal wanderings. But now, the memory replayed in my mind with a new, sinister twist. What if those frantic sounds weren't pleas for entry, but warnings? Warnings I had ignored, blinded by my own self interest and crippling anxieties.

And the strange incidents leading up to her disappearance? The mysteriously misplaced keys, the inexplicably opened window – minor inconveniences then, now chilling clues in a macabre puzzle. Perhaps Mr. Whiskers had been more involved than I'd dared to acknowledge. Perhaps his actions weren't accidental mishaps, but calculated moves in a silent game of feline revenge. A game played with the quiet efficiency only a cat could master.

The detective's words echoed in my mind: "She was a vibrant woman, full of life. It's hard to imagine someone wanting her gone." Hard to imagine, indeed. Unless, of course, that someone was…me. But even my warped perspective couldn't completely reconcile the notion that Mr. Whiskers, my seemingly innocent companion, held a part in the scheme.

His eyes, usually pools of amber tranquility, held a glint, an almost imperceptible spark that I hadn't noticed before. A spark of intelligence, perhaps, or something darker, something colder. He had always been observant, a silent witness to my every flaw, my every fear, my every descent into madness. Now, it occurred to me that his silence might have been less about passivity and more about calculated strategy.

I recalled a childhood memory, a vague, half-forgotten incident. A prized possession, a small wooden toy, gone missing. The only suspect: Mr. Whiskers' predecessor, a ginger tabby I fondly (or perhaps foolishly) remembered as Mittens. A meticulous search had yielded nothing, and I'd attributed its disappearance to my own clumsiness. But now…could Mittens have been involved? Was this a recurring pattern, a dark, hereditary trait passed down through generations of feline conspirators?

I shivered, a cold wave of dread washing over me, pushing aside the guilt and self-loathing. The implications were terrifying. Was I merely a pawn in a larger game, a game orchestrated by a creature that understood my weaknesses better than I did myself? Had Mr. Whiskers silently manipulated my actions, pulling the strings from the shadows, guiding me down this dark path? Had he cleverly used my anxieties, my social ineptitude, my crippling fear of connection, to achieve his own inscrutable ends?

The thought was preposterous, yet…intriguing. It offered a perverse comfort, a way to deflect the crushing weight of responsibility. If Mr. Whiskers was the architect of Sarah's disappearance, then I was merely an unwitting participant, a cat's puppet in a sinister play.

The rain outside intensified, drumming against the windows like a frantic heartbeat. Mr. Whiskers, still purring on my lap, looked up at me, his amber eyes gleaming with an unnerving intelligence. He blinked slowly, once, twice. It felt like a knowing glance, a silent acknowledgment of our shared secret. Or perhaps it was just my imagination, twisting reality to fit my desperate need for absolution.

Days blurred into weeks. The police investigation continued, focusing on the ex-boyfriend, a man whose brutal history seemed to fit the narrative far too neatly. The media frenzy subsided, replaced by whispers and speculation. My carefully constructed façade of normalcy remained intact, a fragile shield protecting me from the terrifying truth.

But the purr. That incessant purr, always present, always constant, never quite leaving my ears, held a new undercurrent. It wasn't just a purr anymore; it was a taunt, a mocking reminder of the silent pact we had formed, a pact sealed in shadows and deceit. It was a purr that whispered of secrets and retribution, a chilling symphony of feline vengeance.

One night, while staring at Mr. Whiskers' sleek form, a new detail surfaced in my memory, a flash of movement caught from the corner of my eye. The night Sarah disappeared, I remembered a fleeting image, a black blur darting from the shadows, a flash of dark fur against the moonlight. Not Mr. Whiskers' ginger coat, but something much darker, something…silhouetted.

Had Mr. Whiskers been working with an accomplice? A shadowy feline confederate, a silent partner in crime? The notion was outlandish, almost ludicrous. Yet, it fitted the pattern, the escalating chain of events, culminating in Sarah's disappearance.

Sleep became a luxury I could no longer afford. Nightmares haunted my dreams, filled with shadowy figures and frantic meows. I saw Sarah's face, her eyes filled with a mixture of fear and accusation. But alongside her, a new image appeared: a sleek, black cat, eyes burning with malice, watching, judging, always present.

Was this my imagination or a reflection of a terrifying truth? Had Mr. Whiskers, my supposedly innocent companion, been pulling the strings all along? Was this a carefully orchestrated game of feline revenge, played out on a stage of my own anxieties and self-deception? Or was I, once again, projecting my guilt onto an innocent creature, seeking refuge in a narrative that suited my fractured reality? The truth, as always, remained elusive, hidden beneath layers of paranoia and self-deception. The only constant was the purr, a haunting, relentless melody accompanying my descent into a darkness far deeper than I could have ever imagined. The cat's revenge, it seemed, was not a simple act of violence, but a slow, insidious manipulation, a masterful game played over time, a perfect execution of feline vengeance. The question remained: was it merely a figment of my guiltridden mind or a sinister truth hiding in plain sight, obscured by the purr of an ever-present, ever-watchful companion? The answer, I fear, remained

as elusive and untouchable as the elusive gleam in Mr. Whiskers' watchful eyes.

THE AFTERMATH

The interrogation room's sterile scent, a peculiar blend of disinfectant and despair, clung to me like a second skin. The clock's relentless ticking had become the soundtrack to my unraveling, each second a hammer blow against the fragile edifice of my carefully constructed lies. Detective Miller's departure hadn't brought relief; it had left a void, a chilling emptiness that mirrored the hollowness within me. He hadn't arrested me, not yet, but the unspoken accusation hung heavy, a suffocating weight pressing down on my chest.

My gaze drifted to the wilting lilies, their once vibrant petals now drooping like defeated soldiers. Sarah loved lilies. The irony wasn't lost on me; these flowers, a symbol of her beauty and life, now felt like a morbid testament to her disappearance. A cruel, fragrant epitaph. The image of her, laughing, her eyes sparkling with mischief, flashed before my eyes, a phantom limb in my memory, a painful reminder of what I'd lost, or perhaps, what I'd taken.

Mr. Whiskers, my perpetually aloof feline companion, sat perched on the windowsill, his emerald eyes gleaming with an unnerving intelligence. His purr, usually a comforting drone, now felt like a mocking symphony, a sinister soundtrack to my internal disintegration. Was he truly innocent? Or had I been blind, foolishly attributing my failings to a creature who, in his own silent, feline way, was orchestrating my downfall? The thought, once absurd, now felt chillingly plausible.

The police investigation, I'd learned, had focused intently on Sarah's abusive ex-boyfriend, Mark. The evidence against him was compelling; threatening messages, a history of violence, a plausible motive. The arrest seemed like a satisfying conclusion, a neat resolution to a messy tragedy. But the satisfaction was short-lived, a fleeting illusion shattered by the insidious whispers of doubt gnawing at my conscience.

The truth, as it always had, remained slippery, elusive, a phantom limb I couldn't quite grasp. My narrative, woven with meticulous care, was starting to fray at the edges, unraveling like a cheap sweater in the wash. Had I, in my desperate attempt to avoid facing the consequences of my actions, woven a web of deceit so intricate, so convincing, that even I was beginning to believe it?

The anxiety, a constant companion, was now a raging inferno, consuming everything in its path. The familiar tightness in my chest intensified, my breath shallow and ragged. Each beat of my heart felt like a thunderclap against my ribs, a brutal reminder of my own culpability. The purr, the constant, rhythmic purr of Mr. Whiskers, intensified, its hypnotic quality both soothing and terrifying. Was it a lullaby, or a death knell?

The investigation hadn't unearthed any concrete evidence linking me to Sarah's disappearance, but the police, I sensed, were beginning to suspect. My erratic behavior, my evasiveness, the inconsistencies in my statements—all painted a picture of guilt, a portrait of a man desperately trying to cover his tracks. I'd been careful, meticulously meticulous in my planning, but even the most meticulously crafted lie has its flaws, its telltale cracks that eventually reveal the rotten core within.

The truth, I realized with a sickening lurch in my stomach, wasn't a simple act of violence, a dramatic confrontation. It was a slow, insidious process, a meticulously planned dance of deception where I, the supposedly harmless recluse, was the choreographer, the conductor of this macabre ballet of shadows. Sarah's disappearance wasn't a random act of violence; it was a consequence of my actions, a culmination of my inadequacies and my desperate desire to escape the suffocating weight of my own existence.

My relationship with Sarah had been fragile, tenuous, built on a foundation of unspoken anxieties and hesitant interactions. My awkward attempts at courtship, veiled in my characteristic nervous ramblings, had probably been perceived as bizarre, off-putting. The thought of rejection, the fear of exposure, had fueled my increasingly erratic behavior, pushing me closer to the precipice of despair.

The plan, initially conceived as a desperate attempt to connect, to break through my self-imposed isolation, had spiraled out of control, morphing into something far darker, far more sinister. The initial anxiety morphed into a frenzied concoction of paranoia and fear, driving me to the brink of insanity.

The night of Sarah's disappearance, I'd been consumed by a potent cocktail of fear, resentment, and self-loathing. The frustration, pent up for years, had erupted like a geyser, overwhelming me with a primal urge to obliterate the source of my torment: my own inadequacy, my profound social awkwardness, and the ever-present, judging gaze of Mr. Whiskers.

My cat, ironically, had become the perfect scapegoat. His presence, his aloofness, his ever-present scrutiny had become symbolic of my own anxieties and insecurities. In my warped perception, blaming him had been a defense mechanism, a way to deflect the blame, to avoid confronting the horrifying truth about myself. He was the convenient fall guy, the perfect patsy in my elaborate self-preservation act.

But the truth, a relentless tide, was slowly washing away the layers of my carefully constructed lies. The arrest of Mark, while seemingly bringing closure, felt more like a delaying tactic, a postponement of the inevitable reckoning. The weight of guilt, once bearable, was now crushing, suffocating. I felt exposed, vulnerable, a puppet whose strings had been expertly cut by the master puppeteer of my own creation.

I looked at Mr. Whiskers again. His gaze was unwavering, his emerald eyes gleaming with a disturbing mixture of amusement and disdain. Was it a reflection of my own guilt? Or was he truly orchestrating things from behind the scenes, a feline mastermind pulling the strings of my own demise? The line between reality and perception blurred, the boundaries of my sanity fraying further with each passing moment.

The silence in the interrogation room was deafening, punctuated only by the rhythmic tick-tock of the clock and the unnerving purr of my cat. The lilies, symbols of a love lost, withered further, a chilling mirror of my own decaying moral fiber. The cold seeping into my bones mirrored the coldness that now permanently resided in my heart. There was no escape. The truth, raw and unforgiving, was closing in, ready to swallow me whole. And in the end, it would be my own self-deception, my desperate need to blame another, that would be my ultimate undoing. The cat's revenge, it seemed, was not a simple act of violence, but a slow, insidious manipulation, a masterful game played over time, a perfect execution of feline vengeance. Or was it just my guilt-ridden mind, spinning a narrative of feline retribution to avoid facing the chilling truth? The answer remained elusive, a shadow in the dimly lit interrogation room, as ambiguous and untouchable as the elusive gleam in Mr. Whiskers' watchful eyes. The truth, I realized, was a creature far more elusive than any cat. It was a phantom I'd created, and it was finally catching up to me. The game, it seemed, was over. And I had lost.

A FINAL THOUGHT

The fluorescent hum of the interrogation room lights seemed to mock my predicament. Each flicker was a tiny, malevolent spotlight on the carefully constructed facade I'd maintained for so long. Detective Miller had left, but his skepticism clung to the air, thick and suffocating. He hadn't bought my story, not for a second. He'd seen the cracks in my carefully crafted narrative, the subtle inconsistencies, the barely concealed tremor in my voice when I spoke of Mr. Whiskers.

My cat, the innocent pawn in my twisted game. Or was he?

The purr, a low rumble emanating from the cat carrier beside me, felt strangely menacing. It was a sound I'd once found comforting, a soothing balm to my frayed nerves. Now, it grated on my ears, a constant, insidious reminder of my deception. Mr. Whiskers, with his unnervingly intelligent emerald eyes, had become a symbol, not just of my isolation, but of my self-deception. Had he truly orchestrated everything, or was this a delusion, a desperate attempt to deflect the blame from myself?

The lilies, wilting symbols of my failed connection with Clara, seemed to mirror my own withering morality. Their once vibrant petals, now brown and brittle, were a stark contrast to the pristine white of the interrogation room walls, a stark reminder of the purity I'd so carelessly violated. The irony wasn't lost on me; I, who prized order and control above all else, had created a chaos that I couldn't begin to understand. The meticulously crafted structure of my life, my carefully maintained routines, had crumbled into dust.

They say a cat has nine lives. Perhaps that's why Mr. Whiskers is still so calm, so smug, even now. Perhaps he knows something I don't. Perhaps he orchestrated this whole thing, playing me like a fiddle, a master manipulator hidden behind a façade of innocent feline charm. Or perhaps it's simply my own guilt, my overwhelming anxiety, transforming a series of unfortunate events into a fantastical, self-serving narrative of feline revenge.

The truth, I suspect, lies somewhere in the grey area between these two extremes. A blend of my own failings, my social inadequacies, my crippling anxiety, and perhaps, just perhaps, a touch of feline mischief. Clara's disappearance wasn't a simple accident; it was a consequence of my actions, my omissions, my cowardly retreat into the comforting shadows of my self-imposed isolation. My anxiety, my fear of rejection, had fueled my actions, warping my perception until I was left with nothing but a twisted narrative to justify my guilt.

I remember the day Clara moved in, the nervous flutter in my stomach as I watched her unpack from across the street, a kaleidoscope of muted colours against the sterile backdrop of my beige existence. I'd meticulously planned my approach, every word, every gesture, rehearsed a thousand times in my mind. My plan was foolproof; it should have worked perfectly, resulting in a happy ending. Instead, it all went spectacularly wrong. The carefully constructed scaffolding of my plan collapsed under the weight of my own inadequacy.

The fear of failure, the crushing weight of my social anxieties, propelled me into a state of paralysis. It's a debilitating condition, this anxiety, it creeps into every corner of your life and chokes the joy from your existence. Instead of taking the chance, instead of embracing the possibility of connection, I opted for the insidious comfort of the familiar, the predictable pattern of my reclusive existence.

But even then, in my self-imposed prison, I couldn't find true peace. The silence amplified my fears, the emptiness gnawed at my soul. The routine, once a shield against the outside world, had become a straightjacket. And then, Clara. A bright, vibrant flower in the wasteland of my life. She represented everything I craved – connection, understanding, a way out of my self-imposed exile.

My plan to connect with her, born of desperation and fueled by anxiety, was fundamentally flawed. It was a clumsy, poorly conceived construction built on shifting sands. My attempts at connection were misguided, awkward, and ultimately, self-destructive. The very act of trying to approach her, the culmination of weeks of meticulous planning, ended up sabotaging any chance I had of a meaningful relationship.

It was in the aftermath of my failure, the crushing weight of my missed opportunity, that my mind began to unravel. The cat, Mr. Whiskers, became a convenient scapegoat. His presence, once a source of comfort, now became a symbol of my inadequacy, a focus for my self-directed anger and resentment. It was easier to blame the cat, to project my anxieties and inadequacies onto this innocent creature than to confront my own failings.

The police investigation, with its methodical questioning and persistent skepticism, only served to reinforce my delusion. Each question felt like an accusation, a confirmation of my deepest fears. The arrest of Clara's abusive ex-boyfriend felt like a betrayal, a validation of my own twisted narrative. I had constructed a meticulously detailed false narrative, a masterpiece of self-deception, complete with circumstantial evidence and a plausible explanation that had everyone, including myself, believing it.

The chilling reality, however, is that Mr. Whiskers was not the architect of Clara's disappearance. He is a cat, an animal driven by instinct, not malicious intent. The truth, as it always does, was far more complex and far less satisfying than the comforting, self-serving narrative I'd spun. The truth, in its stark and unforgiving form, reveals my own moral failings, my crippling anxiety, and my cowardly inability to confront the consequences of my actions.

The finality of the situation hangs heavy. The silence of the interrogation room is a cruel symphony of self condemnation. The clock's ticking seems to be counting down to an inevitable reckoning. The purr of the cat, once a source of comfort, is now a constant, unsettling reminder of my own duplicity. The wilting lilies, symbols of a love lost, serve as a painful testament to my own self-destructive tendencies. There is a profound sense of bleakness that accompanies this moment, this realization that everything I'd constructed had crumbled, revealing the flawed individual beneath.

And yet, a sliver of dark humor manages to penetrate the gloom. The irony is not lost on me – the recluse, the man who blamed his cat for all his misfortunes, is ultimately undone not by a cunning feline conspiracy, but by his own crippling anxiety and inability to form a genuine human connection. The ultimate act of feline revenge, it seems, wasn't claws or teeth, but the slow, insidious erosion of my own sanity. Was it my anxiety that drove me to this point, or was it the cat? Or was it simply a perfect storm of human failings and feline apathy that led to this disastrous conclusion? The answer, I suspect, remains forever lost in the shadowed corners of my own tormented mind. The game is over. And I lost, not to a cat, but to myself.

The ultimate villain, it turns out, was me all along.

ACKNOWLEDGMENTS

First and foremost, I must thank my wonderfully dysfunctional cat, Mr. Whiskers, for providing endless inspiration (and hairballs). His unwavering judgment and uncanny ability to knock things over proved invaluable during the writing process. My apologies, of course, for any unintended resemblances to actual felines. Any such similarities are purely coincidental. I also extend my gratitude to the local police department for their... thorough investigation. Their unwavering dedication to solving mysteries, even the ones I inadvertently created, was truly impressive. Finally, a massive thank you to my editor, whose patience and sanity are far superior to my own. You're a saint. Or, at least, a very effective editor.

APPENDIX

This appendix contains supplementary material, mostly irrelevant to the plot but included to add to the overall sense of unnecessary complication and mildly unsettling paranoia that permeates the narrative. Please feel free to skip this section. Seriously, it's just extra stuff.

A detailed diagram of Arthur's apartment layout, including the

precise location of every potential hiding spot.

A collection of Arthur's meticulously documented grocery delivery lists, highlighting his increasingly erratic shopping habits.

A transcript of Arthur's interview with the police, annotated with my insightful and perhaps overly critical commentary.

(real one isn't included. Similarized facsimile due to legal issues)

A series of photographs of Mr. Whiskers, displaying a range of ambiguous expressions that you can interpret however you like.

MR
WHISKERS

MR
WHISKERS

HOME LIFE

Dear Arthur,
Thank you for the love,
warmth, and
endless supply of treats that you
shower upon me. Your gentle
strokes and cozy lap make my
purrs even louder, and your
patient understanding of my
quirky antics fills my days with
joy. Though I may
sometimes act aloof or knock
things off the table, know that
you hold a special
place in my heart. Our bond is
one of a kind, and I am grateful
for every moment we share.
With a grateful purr – Mr.
Whiskers

GROCERY LISTS   :

List 1:

Bread 6

Milk 5

Eggs 5

Butter 6

Tea 7

List 2:

Organic whole grain bread 5

Almond milk 3

Free-range eggs 4

Unsalted butter 4

Chamomile tea 8

List 3:

Gluten-free bread 6

Oat milk 10

Duck eggs 6

Ghee 10

Lavender tea 8

List 4:

Sourdough bread 15

Hemp milk 10

Quail eggs 5

Coconut oil 8 Matcha green tea 15 List 5:

Rye bread 10

Cashew milk 10

Ostrich eggs ½ dozen 20 120.00

Avocado oil 25

Dandelion root tea 20

List 6:

Sprouted grain bread 15

Macadamia nut milk 15

Emu eggs ½ dozen 50 per egg

300.00

Truffle oil 40

Tulsi (Holy Basil) tea 20

List 7:

Einkorn bread 20

Camel milk 25

Pheasant eggs 25 dozen

MCT oil 35

Butterfly pea flower tea 25

List 8:

Activated charcoal bread 20

Goat milk 12

Goose eggs 20

Walnut oil 35

Mushroom coffee 40

List 9:

Keto bread 30

Tiger nut milk 10

Turkey eggs 12

Hemp seed oil 25

Yerba mate tea 20

List 10:

Paleo bread 25

Pea milk 8

Guinea fowl eggs 15

Flaxseed oil 25

Chaga mushroom tea 40 List 11:

Cauliflower bread 20.00

Pistachio milk 12.00

Partridge eggs 25 dozen

Pumpkin seed oil 30.00 Rooibos tea 20.00

List 12:

Seaweed bread 18.00

Hazelnut milk 10.00

Bantam eggs 8.00 dozen

Black seed oil 35.00

Hibiscus tea 20.00

List 13:

Cricket flour bread 25.00

Watermelon seed milk 10.00

Dove eggs 60.00 dozen

Grapeseed oil 20.00

Blue lotus tea 35.00

List 14:

Insect protein bread 20.00

Sunflower seed milk 8.00 Swan eggs ½ dozen 100.00 per egg

600.00

Sea buckthorn oil 40.00

Moringa tea 25.00

List 15:

Algae bread 15

Banana milk 6

Peacock eggs ½ dozen 50.00 per egg

300.00

Camelina oil 20.00 bottle

Kava tea 1 lb 30.00

These lists reflect Arthur's increasing eccentricity and his gradual shift towards more unusual and obscure items, mirroring his growing anxiety and detachment from conventional norms.

Here are some unusual items Arthur might buy for Mr. Whiskers, reflecting his increasing eccentricity and obsession with his cat:

Organic Salmon Pâté

Freeze-Dried Quail Eggs

Gourmet Cat Sushi

CBD-Infused Cat Treats

Cat Wine (Non-Alcoholic) *mazon:

PetWineShop Cat Wine Pawty Pack

Catnip Wine Cat Wine Set for Cats &
Kittens (Liquid Catnip) 29.95

Insect Protein Cat Food

Custom-Made Cat Furniture

Cat Grass Garden Kit

Luxury Cat Bed with Memory Foam

Cat-Safe Essential Oils for Aromatherapy

Interactive Laser Toy with AI

Cat Hammock for Windows

Cat DNA Test Kit

Pet Fountain with Filtered Water

Cat-Specific Probiotics

Organic Catnip Bubbles

Cat Treadmill for Exercise

Pet Camera with Treat Dispenser

Cat-Safe Houseplants

Custom-Made Cat Clothing

These items reflect Arthur's increasing eccentricity and his tendency to project his anxieties and need for control onto his cat, Mr. Whiskers.

Here are some unique toys that Arthur might have bought for Mr. Whiskers, reflecting his increasing eccentricity and obsession with his cat:

Robotic Mouse Toy Migipaws Robotic
Mouse Toy Amazon 18.29

Laser Pointer with Random Patterns

Interactive Ball with LED Lights Amazon 9.99

Cat Puzzle Feeder AllforPaws Puzzle Feeder 25.99
Amazon

Catpool toy with flippy fish 27.99

Automatic Feather Teaser

Motion-Activated Butterfly Toy

Cat Tunnel with Crinkle Sounds Petest Collapisble
Pet tunnell with fringe 35" length 19.99

Catnip Bubbles Kitty Love Bubbles

17.99

Electronic Flopping Fish Toy 2 pack flippy fish
13.99

Cat Wheel for Exercise 48" XL Cat wheel Xtra wide

15.7 480.00

Catnip-Infused Scratching Post

Interactive Treat Dispenser

Cat Tree with Multiple Levels and

Hideouts Wayfair 91' Eliza Solid

Wood Cat Condo Large Cat Tree

Tower Condo 1, 199.00

Smartphone-Controlled Laser Toy

Interactive APP control laser ball

29.99

Catnip-Infused Kick Toy

Hanging Door Bouncer Toy 14.99

Catnip-Infused Wand Toy Interactive Cat Ball with
Sound

Effects

Catnip-Infused Mat with Hidden Toys

These toys reflect Arthur's increasing eccentricity and his tendency to project his anxieties and need for control onto his cat, Mr. Whiskers.

THE INTERVIEW

Detective Miller: Mr. Finch, thank you for coming in. We have a few questions regarding your neighbor, Clara Bellweather. When did you last see her?

Arthur: (nervously) I... I saw her on Tuesday evening. She was walking her dog near the lamppost.
She seemed... happy. I didn't intrude, of course. One must respect another's privacy.

Detective Miller: Did you notice anything unusual about her behavior or anyone she might have been with?
Arthur: No, she was alone. Walking her dog, as I said. She seemed cheerful. I didn't see anyone else around.

Detective Miller: We've found traces of your DNA near her apartment. Can you explain how that might have happened?

Arthur: (stammering) I... I don't know. I sometimes walk around the neighborhood. Maybe I touched something near her place. It's just a coincidence, I swear.

Detective Miller: We also found fibers from a cat toy on Clara's clothing. Do you recognize this toy?

Arthur: (hesitant) Yes, it's... it's Mr. Whiskers' toy.
He... he must have carried it over there. He's very independent, you know. He goes out and does things. I can't possibly account for his every move.

Detective Miller: Mr. Finch, we found Sarah's missing phone in your apartment, hidden under Mr. Whiskers' bed. And there were traces of her blood on your slippers. Can you explain this?

Arthur: (voice cracking) It... it wasn't intentional. It was an accident, a terrible, unforeseen accident. Mr. Whiskers... he distracted me. He knocked over the delivery box, and... and things got out of hand. I tried to control the situation, but it was too late.

Detective Miller: Are you saying the cat is responsible for Clara's disappearance?

Arthur: (desperate) Yes, it was Mittens. I didn't mean for it to happen. It was a confluence of unfortunate circumstances. I was just a witness to a terrible tragedy.

Detective Miller: So, no involvement on your part, Mr. Finch?

Arthur: (shaking) Only as a witness. I didn't do anything. It was the cat. It was always the cat.

GLOSSARY

This glossary defines key terms used in the novel, mostly to emphasize the author's pedantic tendencies and penchant for unnecessary detail. Skip this unless you're really that bored.

Mr. Whiskers: A fluffy, enigmatic feline companion with questionable motives.

Social Anxiety: A debilitating condition that makes interacting with other humans feel like a particularly unpleasant form of torture.

Home Delivery: The lifeblood of Arthur's existence.

Paranoia: A state of mind in which you suspect everyone and everything of conspiring against you, especially that darn cat.

Projection: The psychological defense mechanism that allows you to effortlessly blame your mistakes on others, preferably a furry, non-verbal scapegoat.

REFERENCES

While I have drawn inspiration from various sources, I'd prefer not to cite them directly. The less you know about
my inspiration, the more effectively the dark humor and mystery will work. Trust me on this one.

AUTHOR BIOGRAPHY

The author prefers to remain anonymous, mostly due to a crippling fear of public speaking and an even greater fear of angry readers with pitchforks. Let's just say that I'm a recluse who writes at night, fueled by caffeine and a deep-seated desire to unravel the complexities of human behavior (and blame it on the cat). Any resemblance to real persons, living or dead, is purely coincidental. Or is it? Perhaps you'll never know.